William F. Rock

Winter Gatherings

Poems - written chiefly in his youth

William F. Rock

Winter Gatherings
Poems - written chiefly in his youth

ISBN/EAN: 9783337255503

Printed in Europe, USA, Canada, Australia, Japan

Cover: Foto ©Andreas Hilbeck / pixelio.de

More available books at **www.hansebooks.com**

WINTER GATHERINGS;

Poems,

WRITTEN CHIEFLY IN HIS YOUTH.

BY

WILLIAM FREDERICK ROCK.

London;
PRINTED FOR PRIVATE CIRCULATION.

MDCCCLXVII.

PREFACE.

UPWARDS of forty years ago I came from Devonshire to London in search of fortune. I had then a manuscript book of poems, of which I thought highly ; and, among the many plans which I formed for my future livelihood, that of depending on my pen · was a rather prominent and favourite one. Strong claims on my immediate exertion, however, rendered it necessary to abandon this reliance on my weaker powers, and I was not very slow to perceive that I should have little chance of success in literature.

I accordingly devoted myself to activity in another calling, and I have no reason to regret my choice ; for the steady success which, in this happy land, honest industry usually secures, has always attended me ; and in my forty years of business life I have had time and opportunities for some pleasant relaxations. I have added a little to my manuscript, but, better still, I have been enabled to cheer and assist many good men, and to stay the career of some whom I believed to be bad ones, and I have always been ready to step out from the line, when no better man has offered, to fight for the right in the numerous little battles in which the warfare depends upon the rank and file of society.

I am now sixty-five years of age ; and, concurrent with a renewal of my love for the scenes of my youth in beautiful Devon, a partiality for the rhymes of my boyhood, and those of the few leisure hours which I have since had, comes very forcibly to me.

Fortunately for my purpose, the fondness of a sister has preserved the Poems from which the contents of this book are selected, and I have determined to print a few copies, not for sale, but to present to my friends, and perhaps to a few literary persons, who may tell me whether any of my writing ought to go beyond the pleasant circle of those who love me. Criticism beyond this is scarcely needed. It would be too late to encourage if favourable, or to terrify if adverse.

I have only further to beg the indulgence of any one whom I may have unduly troubled, if the perusal of my book has been wearisome.

W. F. R.

WALBROOK, LONDON,
August, 1867.

CONTENTS.

———

POETIC SITES.

———

FLOWERS.

POEMS.

THE BLIND MAN.

FEELING his way with tapping stick,
  And steps as slow as mine were quick,
I saw an old grey-headed man,
And thus I hailed him as I ran:
" Halloo! my old blind friend, I pray
Move onward, do not stop the way."

" I am not blind," said the old man ;
" I once was blind, and then I ran ;
But since I saw I ran too quick,
I take to walking with a stick."

" Oh fie, old grey-beard, blindman, fie,
I do not like to hear a lie
Even in sport and from the young ;
But oh, how black is falsehood, hung
On a slow-moving, aged tongue ! "

" Sweet youth," replied the tottering sage,
" Thy words revive my drooping age.
Come seat me down."   And then he sighed
And said, " Sit by an old man's side,
And he will tell what 'tis to be
Stone-blind, and what it is to see.

" In days long past I ranged the fields
(What boundless pleasure nature yields !)
The crimson-fringèd daisies sprung
Close to my feet when I was young,
And yellow buttercups were spread
In rich profusion 'neath my tread ;
Glowing dog-roses every bush
Made beauteous with their crimson blush ;
The hawthorn bloom decked each May-bough
With floral silver just as now.
On every bank, o'er all the ground,
Nature spread loveliness around,
She decked with beauty every spot,

And yet, alas, I saw it not!
I did not see the swallow come
Each summer to its English home ;
I heard no music from the air,
Nor saw the soaring skylark there,
Flowers, birds, and all the merry things
That fly about with buzzing wings,
So full of love's blest melody :
All these, alas! were lost on me,
I saw them not! You show surprise!
But for all these I had no eyes."

" O father, father, do not speak
Like this, or else my heart will break.
Alas! how dimly have I seen !
I scarcely know that fields are green ;
The wingèd music of the sky
I've heeded not, yet know not why ;
Like yours, my morn is almost night ;
Oh tell me how you got your sight ?"

" My dear young man, it pleased God
To chasten me with His mild rod ;
The eyes that were no use to me
He closed, and I BEGAN TO SEE !

I never moved my stilled eyelid,
Yet saw each flower that once was hid;
I thought on all the loveliness
Which bloomed when I admired it less;
I paced (in mind) by every hedge,
Lifted each russet tuft of sedge,
Thought on the violets which breathe
Their fragrance from the moss beneath;
Looked up, as if I could see there
The lark sustained in upper air;
Thought of the beauty of each nook;
Read the first page of Nature's book;
Turned my thoughts round this happy ball
Of earth where constant blessings fall,
And a God's goodness saw in all.

" O happy, ever happy day,
When moistened with the mystic clay
My eyes first opened to light's ray;
There is no blindness half so blind
As the cold darkness of the mind,
Which passing through a lovely world,
Sees beauty's banner half unfurled;
Which sees the sun pass through the skies,
Or knows that it must set and rise;

Sees the blest summer and the spring
Give warmth to every living thing ;—
Which views all this, though seen so plain,
With cold neglect, or bold disdain.
O my dear friend, to you is left
The light of which I am bereft ;
Kneel down with me and we will pray :
Grant us, O God, Thy heavenly ray,
That, our eyes opened, we may see
In every good a type of Thee ;
That we may look around and trace
Thy bounteous hand in every place,
And then raise eyes and hearts above,
And thus repay Thee love for love."

———

THE COTTAGER'S ADDRESS TO THE MORNING STAR.

"Behold, the sun, and the moon, and the eleven stars made
obeisance to me."—GEN. xxxviii. 9.

STAR of the morning, tellest thou of day ?
Sweet is the visit of thy silvery ray,
        A gentle bud of light,
        More beautiful than bright.

Thou light'st the path of the pale dawn's first hours,
Liftest the drooping eyelids of the flowers,
     And breathest musical words
     To wake the sleeping birds.

I hear their chirpings from the leafy wood,
A twitter first, and then a swelling flood
     Of gratitude to Him
     Who claims their morning hymn.

Delicious Star!   Thy twinkling from above
Awakes the flowers to smiles, the birds to love ;
     And when all else has smiled,
     Thou call'st thy favourite child.

Then Man awakes!   The sovereign of the whole,
Creation's lord, the creature with a soul!
     He wakes to life—to thought
     Which worlds could not have bought.

He wakes, and looks around, below, above ;
All is for him, and all is bright with love,
     And his swoll'n heart is full,
     All is so beautiful.

And then he wonders at creation's plan,
Who could have formed the earth, and seas, and man?
   And his knee meets the sod,
    While his lips breathe forth " God!"

Yet thought will wander, and he heaves a sigh
At the reflection that he still must die,
   And all this beauty leave
    Perhaps before the eve.

Still, thought flows on.   Yes, man indeed will fade,
Returning to the dust whence he was made;
   But wherefore should he sigh,
    His soul can never die.

Star of the Morning, shine, and wane and shine,
More fixed than thou, eternity is mine:
   Yes, Man is nobler far
    E'en than the MORNING STAR!

THE COTTAGER'S ADDRESS TO THE EVENING STAR.

"The star that bids the shepherd fold."—MILTON.

BRIGHT Evening Star ! my harbinger of rest,
The spot where thou first twinklest must be blest :
My own dear family sun,
My toil I see is done.

Blest star, if worlds indeed around thee move,
They must be worlds of bliss—be worlds of love ;
For rest to us thou bringest,
And love's sweet song thou singest.

At thy first glimmer in the soft'ning sky,
Brown Labour smiles and lays his mattock by ;
And Youth looks up to see
The eye of love in thee.

When the bright beams of day begin to leave
For the soft twilight of the love-fraught eve,
Spell-bound, I scarce can turn
From where thy beauties burn.

At thy calm smile the city's voice grew dim,
The little lark, too, ceased its vesper hymn,
  And Echo, in its pride,
  Repeated it and died.

Silence is born of thee, and speech is still,
Though eloquence the bursting heart may fill ;
  The voice of love alone,
  Sweet sparkler, is thy own.

Thou shinest o'er thy cotter's home, sweet star,
Where all his hopes and all his pleasures are ;
  All but one spot is dim
  To point that out to him.

A needless task ! for what is all beside
The tender pleasures of our own fireside ?
  What luxury, what bliss,
  To have a spot like this !

My wife's sweet welcome at my cottage door,
My little prattlers meeting me before,
  What more can riches give ?
  The richest can but live.

Shine, lovely one ! Oh twinkle as before,
And though thou canst not give thy cotter more,
  Shine on, and mayst thou see
  Each cotter blest like me !

————

PARADISE TREE

(NEAR BIDEFORD, DEVON).

"Not only famous but of that *good* fame,
 Without which glory's but a tavern song."—BYRON.

HOW many a summer's sun
 Has danced thy leaves upon !
How often the night zephyrs sighing
Have set thy bunched honours a-flying !
  For a tree more fair
  Never waved in the air,
Nor perhaps more gracefully twined a bough,
Than thine, so shrivelled and wrinkled now.

There garlands perhaps have hung,
And woodland songsters sung,
And lovers have sat and sighed
That the moon its beam might hide,

And a moment's relief
To darken thy leaf
Has been seized on by them for a rapturous kiss,
No witness but thou to their innocent bliss.

Perhaps thou wert part of a wood,
And hast all thy tall neighbours outstood,
And while, like " the lords of the ground,"
They were nodding and falling around,
The roots of thy birth
Grew more fast to the earth ;
And, though not so green, thou art standing as stern
As if thou wert still unexpecting thy turn.

I can fancy that under thy shade
The pipe and the fiddle have played,
While round thee in fairy-like ring
The youth of the village would fling ;
For fame must be wrought,
Or 'tis quickly forgot ;
And how many a heart must have bounded with glee
To earn thee the sweet name of " PARADISE TREE ! "

Oh, that story, old Stump, should withhold
These tales of the pleasures of old ;

If the joys of these times are so few,
Come, give us the old ones anew,
  Or I in my rhyme
  Will sing of the time
When the lads and the lasses at eve came to thee,
And danced in the shade of old Paradise Tree.

"I was reared then"—Hark! hark! "I was reared—
But age has my memory seared;
Yet many have shaken my bough
Whose faces I never see now,
  And I tremble to hear
  The names still so dear,
Now talked of as heading a funeral stone,
While the villagers weep for my friends that are gone.

"I have heard the soft sighs of the heart,
I have felt of each sorrow a part,
I have heard the loud laugh 'neath my boughs,
Which shook with the joyous carouse;
  The wanderer's feet
  Have turned to my seat,
And in storm and in sunshine for ever were free
The shade and the shelter of Paradise Tree.

"I've administered oft to the mirth
Of the village to which I owe birth;

Given shade 'mid the summer day's toil,
And added at eve to their smile ;
    Nor did I withhold,
    When the winter blew cold,
A straggling branch from the shivering poor,
And what could the Lord of the Manor do more ?

" My young boughs have waved in the air
When beauty and freshness were there,
And now when the wintry wind
Has bleached and disfigured my rind,
    Enjoying the fame
    Of a well-acquired name,
I can smile at the crowds who only are known
By their name on a half-decayed mouldering stone.

" But what shall I say to the one
Who admires me when beauty has gone,
When the dark howling wintry blast
Has withered my top as it passed ?
    I have nought to repay,
    For I fall to decay,
But softly my ashes shall crumble o'er thee,
If they bury thee under old Paradise Tree."

A DAY AT INSTOW, DEVON.

I SPENT a day, oh ! such a day,
    Why will such moments pass away ?
Pure joy, I think, should ever stay.

I was in Devon, on the marge
Of two clear rivers ; neither large,
Their freshets scarcely float a barge.

But each can boast a foaming tide
So deep that safely there may ride
Large ships, the mighty ocean's pride.

Wild Dartmoor gives one stream its source,
Wending round pleasant woods its course,
From each hill-brook it gathers force.

The TAW, my own loved native stream,
Is worth a water-poet's dream ;
It is a floating sunshine beam.

Whether it lifts its tiny moans
In leaping over boulder stones,
Or tinkles with more silver tones ;

Or passing Tawstock's verdant wood,
At Barum meets the upward flood,
And shows the town its river god.

The TORRIDGE, child of the moors too,
At first as small as dropping dew,
Soon soaks a crystal passage through

The bog, the sheep-paths, the roadside,
(Where sunburnt maidens' ponies ride,)
And finds its daisied margin wide.

For having left its ridgy Tors,
And the adjoining sheep-cropped moors,
It soon its rain-fed ripples pours,

And gives its name to a fair town ;
Then, wider spreading, topples down
Through grassy meads in channels brown.

Still wider grown, the Torridge rill,
Passing Weir Gifford's manse and mill,
Takes shadows from Malclevi's hill.

Then leaves its rural banks of sedge,
And leaping Ford's old stepping-ridge,
Sweeps through the many-archèd bridge.

Well—these two streams their wanderings o'er,
Just as they go, to be no more,
Join their bright floods at Appledore.

And opposite that port marine,
At once a sea and sylvan scene,
Sits Instow, like a river queen ;

Rich in its sands and fishers' hooks,
And daisied hills and cottage nooks,
As poets will describe, in books.

There our dear " Invalided " lay,
And wrote us how that day by day
Health chased her pallid looks away.

And so I said, " Well, I will go
Where these health-bearing breezes blow ;
I'm off !—aye, whether I can or no."

I Instow reached and smiled, and said,
" God bless you, the pale cheeks are fled,
And once again, dear, they are red :

And as you are not very weak,
And I have only just a week,
Each day we must some pleasure seek."

But this I scarcely need have said,
For plans enough were ready laid,
Though I a dozen weeks had stayed.

Well, for our day. We rose at seven,
And saw, of course, a sunny heaven,
For which and all our thanks were given.

I, before breakfast, sallied forth,
And knew the place from south to north,
And every man's and woman's worth.

Then after coffee, milk, and eggs,
And thin-sliced tongue, and chickens' legs,
We filled the hamper and the kegs.

And at that moment came along
Our boatman, with a snatch of song;
With him the wind is never wrong.

" Well, William! how about the boat? "
" Plaise, Mim, 'tis jist agot afloat,
An' I've the oars an' zails abrought."

Ten minutes placed us in our seats,
And in the midships drinks and meats,
And little knick-knacks, fruits and sweets.

And, as we wished, the fair winds blew,
And as we tacked the winds tacked too,
Just as they usually do.

With pleasant tales and hearty joys,
And laughs, and songs, and such sweet noise,
We passed by all the pilot buoys.

William declared a sweet-toned gale
From every song swelled out his sail
(Such winds at Instow must prevail).

Full soon " the pebble ridge " we reach,
Running our shallop on the beach,
We landed with a load for each.

Piling our stores on the sand-banks,
We then began to play our pranks,
Through drifted sand and tall sedge ranks ;

Now looking at a dark sea-mew,
Now listening to the wild curlew,
Or stepping little sea-pools through.

And then we gathered tiny cells,
Of sea things, many-coloured shells,
Thrown up from ocean's briny wells;

And wondered why such lovely forms
Were given as houses for such worms;
And talked of calms and talked of storms.

And then we looked at distant sails,
And wondered where they met with whales;
And now and then glimpsed rabbits' tails.

And then leaped over rifted rocks,
And stranded rudders, yards, and blocks,
And saved a bit to make a box.

And every now and then we met
Sea-dabs and weeds above the wet,
And varied stones from milk to jet.

And searching, as we sauntered on,
We now and then selected one,
And thought the last the brightest shone.

And here and there we caught a glimpse
In rock-pools of those little imps,
The savoury morsels we call shrimps.

And then I said, " You here may rest,
Until I yonder am undrest ;
I will the foamy ocean breast.

" Five minutes will be ample quite,
I shall be nearly out of sight,
And only seem a speck of white.

" Then see me in the salt sea lave,
And battle with the mountain wave,
And talk of manhood and the brave."

Well ! this passed too.   We look abroad,
And see along the sandy road
Our boatman struggling with his load.

We run, with pleasure in our eyes,
And each a little help supplies,
And soon unpacked are joints and pies.

Stones form our table and our seat,
Pebbles confine our napkin neat ;
And thus might princes drink and eat.

Then on the sand supine we lie,
Looking right up into the sky,
All thoughtless and luxuriously ;

Just deeming that those pretty things
That bask in sunbeams their gauze wings,
Might lessons give to queens and kings.

But this, you know, would only do
Just for a warm half-hour or two,
Not for the afternoontide through.

So after just a little snooze,
We thought us of our homeward cruise,
And even hinted evening's dews.

William had left us but light work ;
We packed each napkin, knife and fork,
And played at balls with every cork.

But ere we left the hallowed ground,
One song from each was sung around,
And off we sprang with merry bound.

Since then, in London's noisiest throng,
The echo of each simple song
Oft floats the busy din among.

Distinct above the varied noise
Which marks the struggle for life's toys,
It sings, " How cheap are harmless joys ! "

THE RUINED TEMPLE.

" He spake of the temple, his body."
" The temple of the Lord is holy, which temple ye are."

LOOK at yon fane where ruin sits,
 Where serpents twine and the bat flits,
 Where noxious weeds grow high and rank,
 Concealing pits obscene and dank.

This was a temple fair and bright,
Glowing with pure and heavenly light,
A temple of the living God,
Which nothing base or sinful trod.

Once holy love and fervent prayer,
From morn to silent night were there,
And every virtue of the mind
Was in this temple once enshrined.

There dwelt the ever-blessed three,
Pure Faith, and Hope, and Charity;
And God Himself, with special grace,
Made it His own bright dwelling-place.

O favoured temple ! glorious shrine !
O dwelling-place thus made divine !
What ruined thus the bright abode
Of the supreme, eternal God ?

In evil hour a fatal sin
Knocked at the door and entered in,
And spread around its loathsome breath,
Drawn from the charnel-house of death.

The power of darkness chased away
The shining spirits of the day ;
Faith, Hope, and Charity all fled,
And left Despair and Hate instead.

Then love in lust unholy burned,
And soberness to riot turned,
And stern defiance, doubts and fears
Came, but no penitential tears.

The *oratory* gave no sigh,
But deep-mouthed oath or ready lie ;
The *altar* had its garlands torn,
Which were as sinful trophies worn.

The *lattice*, whence Love used to look,
Unholier spirits conquering took;
The *Tower of Heshbon* tumbling came,
Pulled down by Guilt's debasing shame.

What could the Great Eternal do,
But, still to purest virtue true,
Leave the foul ruin as it fell,
To the congenial powers of hell?

High o'er the ruin Satan cowers,
The fatal conquest of his powers,
Boasts of a temple won from heaven,
And to his fell dominion given.

The howl of darkness and despair
Thence pours to him a fitting prayer,
And brimstone censers there he lights,
In mockery of holier rites.

But Mercy, from its bright abode,
Stoops, with an offer yet from God;
Awakens Hope, still lingering there,
Which whispers in it yet a prayer.

'Twas but for mercy, one deep sigh,
But see ! Despair and Anguish fly :
The temple's echoing walls are full—
" The Lord our God is merciful ! "

The holy altar smokes again,
Not with the blood of bullocks slain ;
A contrite heart upon it lies,
And God accepts the sacrifice.

O wondrous temple ! living fane !
Bright dwelling-place of God again !
Thence daily shall fresh incense rise,
With prayer and penitential sighs.

Till, consecrate in perfect love,
Incorporate with thy church above,
Restored, this temple, Lord, shall be ;
Builded, raised up, and blent with Thee.

THE ENCHANTER'S GLASS.

COME, come, Enchanter, prithee pass
The earth's bright phantoms o'er thy glass ;
Come, show me what the world can give
To one who wishes well to live.

The scene is sweet ;—a joyous child ;
Its crowing laugh, its tendril fingering,
Like a young vine-shoot running wild,
Clinging to all, yet nowhere lingering.
O Childhood ! happy, blithe, and free,
I will choose thee ; yes, I'll choose thee.

Yet pass this scene.   Thou canst show more,
Enchanter, by thy magic lore ;
Prithee my pulse more wildly move
With deeper scenes.   I would see Love.

What's this ?   Ah ! love indeed is here ;
No one can doubt that faithful greeting,
Its joy, its still more precious tear,
The tear of parting—aye, of meeting,
When love's cup overflows with bliss.
I will choose this ; I will choose this.

Again shift on thy figures, Seer,
The world's great gifts do not appear ;

I would view one who has been hurled
Amidst the bustling busy world.
    I see! Yon struggler leaps and tries
To reach the golden prize hung o'er him ;
    He gains it! See, the good and wise
Bow down their care-bleached heads before him.
'Tis well—how can it be amiss
To o'ertop all ?—I will choose this.

Thy shadows, Seer, again pass on,
I still would see a nobler one,
One who can boast a titled name
High on the glittering roll of fame.
    Ah, there he is! without a scar,
He has the homage of a nation,
    A medal, garter, cross, and star—
The highest rank, the proudest station.
Well, this *is* brave. No one, I wis,
Can e'er condemn if I choose this.

O Seer, my weary spirits pant
For something I seem yet to want ;
The little phantoms of thy glass
Are all forgotten as they pass.

What is this scene ?   In bold relief
A bowed-down figure I am seeing,
  A man of sorrows and of grief.
O God ! it is that Precious Being ;
Sorrow with Him appears such bliss,
I will choose this, I will choose this.

Sorrow for sin.   There is no part,
In earthly or in heavenly heart,
So good, so Godlike, or so pure,
So bright, so lasting, or so sure.
  But whence these tears in Him who spread
The great and glorious heaven above me ?
  Oh, can it be ?   His tears thus shed
Because I sin.   Can He still love me ?
Oh let me mingle mine with His !
Sorrow for sin.   I will choose this !

"IT IS I, BE NOT AFRAID !"

CEASE, timid soul, each agonizing sigh,
  Be every fear, be every doubt allayed ;
Dread not the storm which howls along the sky,
The Spirit that controls the storm is nigh.
                "'Tis I, be not afraid !"

Does sin assail, thy wavering faith to try;
  By Me, thy staff, thy fallings shall be stayed;
Look but on Me the evil one will fly;
Fear not, thou little one, for I am nigh.
          " 'Tis I, be not afraid!"

Say, hast thou fallen?   Thou meet'st no angry eye,
  Since thou repentest, I will not upbraid;
Enough one tear, one penitential sigh;
I knew the trial, how, and when, and why.
          " 'Tis I, be not afraid!"

Does sickness bow thee, does the grave seem nigh,
  Does heaven not brighten as earth 'gins to fade?
Cheer up, poor doubter, time is passing by;
Repose in holy confidence—" 'Tis I."
          " 'Tis I, be not afraid!"

THE MONARCH'S ENTRY.

" Fear not, daughter of Zion, behold thy King cometh."
JOHN xii. 15.

LIFT up your head, great Salem's gate,
  Welcome your Victor-monarch home;
The King of Jewry and His state
  In new and mighty triumph come!

Ten thousand voices move the air,
   And the loud plaudits fill the sky,
Ten thousand bosoms beat their prayer—
   Hosanna to the Lord most High!

The multitude have strewn the way
   As ne'er was Conqueror's pathway spread,
No boughs of laurel or of bay,
   Ensanguined types of life blood shed;
But the green palm-branch speaking peace
   To all on earth, goodwill to men;
Tells of the time when war shall cease,
   And lambs lie in the lion's den.

The Victor comes!   His captives, see,
   Follow in meek array His train;
His captives, those whom He makes free!
   Enfranchised souls from Satan's chain.
The proud, by meekness low subdued,
   In full submission now lie down;
The meek, with holy hopes endued,
   Look up and ask and share His crown.

The blind whom He hath made to see,
   The lame whom He hath made to go,

His triumph join. With new-born glee
  The lame man leapeth like the roe;
The deaf awake to sounds unused,
  They hear the wide-resounding cry;
The dumb speak out, their tongues now loosed,
  Hosanna to the Lord most High.

Jerusalem receives her King,
  The mighty Monarch mounts His throne,
Uplifted high! Strange triumphing!
  For see, His sacred blood hath flown ;
Suspended on the fatal tree,
  In death His holy head bows down
In solitary majesty,
  For all His followers have flown.

He triumphs yet. Borne to the tomb,
  The stone is sealed and watched in vain,
The grave itself is but the womb
  Whence God and man are born again.
Death hath surrendered now its sting,
  No more victorious is the grave,
A mightier realm now claims its King,
  A countless throng their Monarch crave.

The sky unwonted glory wears,
   Filled with a bright angelic train;
The new Jerusalem appears,
   And Jesus here is King again.
Lo! He ascends! Our eyes in vain
   Would view the wonders of above;
Commenced is the Eternal Reign,
   The Reign of Glory, Goodness, Love.

THE KIND MASTER.

"My yoke is easy, and my burden is light."—MATTHEW xi. 30.

LOOK around upon the busy world,
   And see an anxious and a struggling throng
So sad, it seems as though a curse were hurled
   Upon each victim as he moves along.

The sunken eye, the wrinkled brow of care,
   The quivering lip and the upheaving breast,
The gasping breath, the ever-ready tear,
   The unsteady pulse, a stranger to all rest.

What breeds this tumult, and what means this din ?
   What demon guides them, or what tyrants drive ?
Can ill from good proceed ? When days begin
   Must sin and sorrow with the light arrive ?
Alas ! man, self-enslaved, no more retains
   The mighty freedom of his early days ;
The slave of many masters hugs his chains,
   And pride and passion he by turns obeys.

Hard taskers they. At their too stern demands
   Joy and Content take wing, e'en Wisdom flies.
At Mammon's altar, Truth a victim stands ;
   Virtue and Hope complete the sacrifice.
What is this idol-worship, that we bow
   Our abject forms to lick the monster's dust ?
Who thus delights to see his slaves so low ?
   "The Good," "the Wise," "the Mighty," or "the Just"?

Ah, no ! It is the god of *this* world claims
   Such fearful homage from his trembling slaves ;
'Tis Satan's vassals who thus work in chains,
   Till pain and anguish sink them to their graves.
Oh, can it be, that, deaf to reason's voice,
   From grace, from mercy, from redeeming love,
Man turns away and makes a fatal choice,
   Grovelling below, when he might soar above ?

D

Another Master would his soul engage,
    The yoke is easy, and the burden light;
Eternal glory is the offered wage,
    A home unfading and companions bright.
Come, sin-encumbered, throw thy burden down!
    Come, over-wearied, come to Him and rest!
The low, the abject, yet may wear a crown;
    The doomed, the fallen, the helpless, yet be blessed!

He calls! His gracious promises invite
    To joy, to happiness, the guilty throng;
Serve Him with gladness, in His law delight,
    And come before His presence with a song.
No gloomy service His. A joy supreme
    Pervades each heart that puts its trust in Him;
Immortal goodness is the constant theme,
    Eternal praises the unceasing hymn.

Oh, come, be blest! Risk not an hour's delay;
    Leave this world's gods, idols of stock and stone,
With heads of gold and feet of miry clay,
    And serve the Lord Omnipotent alone!
The Great, the Gracious Giver of all good
    Withholds no bounty, and denies no care;
For gifts, the Giver asks but gratitude,
    For hope, for grace, for mercy, but a prayer.

ROBIN OF AYR.

I HAD a blessèd dream last night ;
    I slept with moonbeams for my pillows,—
Such moonbeams as, with silver light,
    Tip and smooth down the summer billows.
I lay, though soul-entranced, awake ;
    Or, if asleep, in softest slumbers ;
No spring-bird's music from the brake
    Could match my fancy's pleasant numbers :
        I heard my Robin, our own dear Robin,
        Our ricketty-racketty, own dear Robin!
No linnet or thrush, from blossoming bush,
    E'er sang like our own dear high-souled Robin.

I looked up and the sky was light,
    And full of happy, joyous creatures,
And 'mid the brightest of the bright
    I saw dear Robin's well-known features
Foremost among the glittering throng ;
    He looked so white, and fair and pure,

D 2

I scarcely knew our child of song,
　　He stood so calm and so demure.
　　　　But there was Robin, our own dear Robin,
　　　　Our ricketty-racketty, own dear Robin!
Not his daisy bright with its vermeill'ed white
　　Could look more pure than our own dear Robin.

I said, "Why, Robert, can that be you?
　　How came ye, my lad, that long white robe in?"
Qnoth he with a smile that quite warmed me through,
　　"From Time's first day it was made for Robin;
The world only saw me in ploughman's dress,
　　Spattered and soiled by the crowd I moved in;
It has since been cleaned of its mire and mess,
　　But it's the very robe I lived and loved in."
　　　　Oh, dear Robin! loving Robin!
　　　　My ricketty-racketty, own dear Robin!
There's never a king that poet could sing
　　That had such a robe as this dear Robin!

"But how did you manage, dear Robert," said I,
　　"To atone for your faults?   You've been punished, I'm
　　　　thinking:
Very often folk say of you, Rob, with a sigh,
　　'Oh what has become of Rob's roving and drinking?'"

Robin said : "Don't you know in this glorified sphere
   There's no such debasement as tippling and roving,
Good fellowship turns to communion here,
   And our constant employment is to keep loving.
      Yes, your Robin, your own dear Robin,
      The once so ricketty-racketty Robin,
Still sings the same tune, as by Ayr and by Doon,
   He is still the same heart-throbbing, love-breathing
   Robin!"

"THIS IS AS IT SHOULD BE."

(The last words of DOUGLAS JERROLD.)

THE time speeds on when we must go
   From all who love us, all we love!
The hour will have its share of woe,
   However blest the change may prove ;
However bright heaven's opening skies,
   Although we may both great and good be,
Affection's tears will dim the eyes,
   And this is as it should be.

Oh, who unweeping and unwept
    Would leave a world so fair as this,
Which when he woke and when he slept
    Had still love's look, love's smile, love's kiss ;
Where wife, child, sister, brother, friend
    Were loving, aye, as fond hearts could be—
Love lasting on unto the end!
    Oh this is as it should be !

Raised, gently raised by some kind hand,
    Leaning on some dear, loving breast,
Surrounded by the close-linked band,
    Our hand by some hand fondly pressed ;
Hearing the half-suppressèd sighs,
    As gently breathed as anguish could be,
Looking on tear-suffusèd eyes ;
    Oh this is as it should be !

O precious sighs !   O joyous tears !
    O grief that almost hallows feeling !
O glorious hopes !   O needful fears,
    Salvation's wondrous plan revealing !
Weep, dear ones ! weep as Jesus wept
    For one He loved.   Wept let the good be,
But be not grief's bounds overstepped ;
    Let all be as it should be.

Come, sweet remembrances of all
　　The tenderness which marked their living ;
Yes, let our memories recall
　　Our frequent faults, their warm forgiving:
Then one long thought, that they must now
　　With countless myriads of the good be;
That when we meet again we know
　　All will be as it should be.

"NOW I SHALL GO TO SLEEP."

(The last words of BYRON.)

" It was about six o'clock on the evening of this day when he said, 'Now I shall go to sleep,' and then turning round fell into that slumber from which he never awoke."—*Moore's Notices of the " Life of Byron."*

NOW I shall go to sleep. Oh yes, my day of life is o'er ;
　The sun which shortly now will set will rise to me no more;
What I have earned I now shall gain, what I have sown
　　shall reap ;
I cannot add unto my work, now I shall go to sleep.

If I have never done as I would others did to me,
Or if unheeded I have heard the voice of misery,
If I have caused the orphan's sigh or made the widow weep,
Who knows what troublous dreams may come now that I go
　　to sleep ?

I fear not this, but yet would live, for there is much to do,
For crime pollutes the trembling earth and murder stalks it
　　through ;
My fluttering heart still leaps to think of some all-glorious
　　deed,
Of oppressors to be vanquished, or of captives to be freed.

And since in my brief day of life, which now I know is past,
I did as I desire to do in this which is my last ;
Over the ceasing of my works a grateful land * shall weep,
And its true tears shall sanctify the ground in which I sleep.

"TÊTE D'ARMÉE !"

(The last words of NAPOLEON BUONAPARTE.)

STRETCHED on a couch the stunted " Conqueror " lies,
　　Not as of yore with rich embroideries,
　　Imperial purple, specked with golden bees,
But on a humble bed he, captive, dies.

* Greece.

The Eagle that once took its awful swoop
    Over its fields of victims, kings its prey,
    Has had of carnage its too-lengthened day,
And now is cabined in a pullet's coop.

But still the wayward mind is fluttering o'er
    The sickening quarry of its hunted things,
    Gloating o'er bleeding, weltering, festering kings,
And glutting its rank appetite with gore.

Worn, wasted, weak the frame, and dull the eyes,
    Languid the limbs, and scant the fevered breath ;
    The scorched-up lip is scarred, but e'en in death
Defiance takes the place of fitter sighs.

Mercy's sweet angel from the horrid bed
    With undelivered message flew at last :
    She waited long. Her final moment passed,
And one fresh fiend sprang from a man now dead:

Th' ambitious spirit as it left its shell
    Shrieked with exulting ardour, "Tête d'Armée ! "
    One withering shout of devils' mockery,
Derisive laughter shook the vaults of hell.

" Tête d'Armée ? "   Oh no ! a mightier one ;
    SATAN, a master mind, is ruler here !
    Down to the common ranks of guilt and fear :
Thy poor ambition's past !   Low fool, thy task is done.

WRITTEN IN AMERICA.   A.D. 1838.

I WALK by mighty Hudson's stream,
    Tread lands beyond the Atlantic sea,
The distance is but as a dream,
    It seems my fatherland to me ;
I listening sigh, for all around
    The small birds' music fills the air ;
How can I deem it foreign ground ?
    Why, all my well-known flowers are here.

I look, and meet a brother's face,
    I am my kindred folk among ;
I speak not to a foreign race,
    They answer in my native tongue ;
I walk into the house of God,
    And they address the self-same prayer ;
I view the neighbouring burial sod,
    The kindred dust commingles there.

I tread the quays, and side by side
   The states' and island's ships are ranged ;
I scan the laws, my loved isle's pride,
   They are, except in form, unchanged ;
I view their stage, and high o'er all
   Our Shakespeare fills the honoured place ;
To genius kindred spirits fall ;
   Can such be deemed a foreign race ?

Great nation, deem us brothers then,
   And grasp the hand a land extends ;
View all the world as fellow-men,
   View us as kinsmen, brothers, friends ;
The same in language, manners, laws,
   Let us in kindness pledge our troth ;
Ours surely is a common cause ;
   Who injures one must injure both.

Our ripened institutions lend
   To you their sanctity and name,
And, rich heir-looms, to you descend,
   Purchased by many a deathless fame :
Drawing your origin from us,
   And fed with such immortal food,
Born, nursed, enriched, ennobled thus,
   What *can* ye be, but great and good ?

And should your Parent Island fall,
  As Greece and Rome have fallen before,
May you her GIANT CHILD, recall
  The shade of greatness then no more,
Catch the bright spirit ere it flies,
  Ere a dark gloom around is hurled,
Purge out its few impurities,
  And give it perfect to the world !

NIAGARA.

TO look upon Niagara !   How long
  That wish had nestled in my inmost breast !
For I had read of it in poet's song,
  And, loving Nature best when lowliest drest,
  I longed to see her in her Monarch-vest,
Her garb of homely beauty laid aside,
  Yet feared to think which I might love the best,
The lowly streamlet of the hillock's side,
Or the great foaming mass of waters in their pride.

And now I hear the distant torrent's roar
  A full, deep, rumbling and incessant sound,
Like when the ground-sea lashes England's shore,
  As if 't would move the rocks which hedge her round ;

(Fit guardians of that blest, that holy ground ;)
And now a vapour-pillar points the site
   Where from its channel the vast stream must bound,
And the great river hastens from my sight
To go it knows not where ; yet powerless is its might,

On it must flow! and not in stealthy streams,
   With pace unnoted, as it flowed of yore,
But with face ruffled to a thousand seams,
   Which pointed rocks, jagged and uneven tore,
   Struggling it passes, clinging to the shore ;
But soon, its wave-worn channel sinking low,
   It rushes onward with impetuous roar,
Driven to the brink by its time-waging flow,
And takes its awful plunge into the gulf below.

Come, let me view the wonder ! let me look
   On Nature, in her grandeur and her power,
Reading the fairer portions of her book,
   I may have missed her in her solemn hour.
   Seeking fresh beauty in each wildling flower,
And melody in every woodland song,
   I have not seen her when her features lower,
Or known the terrors that to God belong,
Not viewing, in His might, the terrible, the strong.

Come, let me look into the great abyss ;
　　See the great rush, " the whirlwind " and " the storms ;"
Hear the vast din where oceans " howl and hiss,"
　　And fell destruction loveliness deforms.
　　Where is the horror which so much alarms,
At which alike timid and strong turn back ?
　　I hear no howls, I see no horrid forms,
Nor dream of nations', or of nature's wrack ;
I see a mighty, but a lovely cataract.

No terrors sit upon its smiling brow,
　　There sunshine plays upon the waters clear,
And as it pours its mighty flood below,
　　Sunshine and glory make their dwelling there.
　　I wonder and admire, but cannot fear,
All is so lovely and so beautiful.
　　See, the blest bow of many tints is here,
A sevenfold bow, with promised safety full,
Spanning the glorious whole, each rising fear to lull.

In floods of grandeur and of love combined,
　　Here Goodness sits upon a godlike throne,
A glorious type of the Eternal Mind,
　　Which tim'rous mortals fear to think upon,

So much of majesty around is thrown,
The gazer fears to raise his eye above:
But as the awe-struck wonderer gazeth on,
The misty veil and shrinking fears remove,
Showing one glorious flood of beauty and of love.

Pour on for ever, thou almighty flood,
Thy stream of goodness thus; for ever flow,
Unchanging emblem of infinitude,
Nor deem thy bounty needs a course more slow;
Unmeasured fountains pour their wealth below,
Where diamond wells in deep concealment lie,
And constant streams that never ebb can know,
For ever flowing bring their rich supply,
Fed by eternal springs—springs that can never dry.

Flow on, Niagara! For ever flow
In power supreme, with peerless beauty bright;
Flow thus for ever, that the world may know
How greatness and how goodness may unite
In beauty perfect, and unmatched in might;
Wielding eternal power with Godlike arm,
On thee securely rests the enraptured sight:
No shrinking dread, no fears of wrong alarm,
Thy glorious power subdues and awes us but to charm.

Still on thy rocks, capped by the mountain pine,
  May flowers of humbler growth their beauties show,
In rich festoons still hang the wildling vine,
  And the red rose and orange lily blow,
  Whilst lowlier grass and countless mosses grow
On the vast footsteps of thy giant throne,
  And, fed by dews which ever fall below,
Boast an eternal verdure all their own,
Which the enchanted sight delights to rest upon.

Pour on, Niagara, for ever pour
  Thy treasure-flood and all around thee bless ;
Thy diamond gifts in ceaseless bounty shower,
  Enriching all, and yet thy store no less ;
  Flow on, and let th' admiring world confess,
No bounds thy beauty or thy bounty knows ;
  Blest shrine, where undeluded pilgrims press,
While each an offering on thy altar throws,
  Blessing the mighty Source from which all glory flows.

THE SPIRIT OF THE YOUNG MAN'S HOME.

THRICE happy Spirit, who doth preside
  Over the young man's blest fireside ;
  Who all his earthly cares beguileth,
  And round his happy circle smileth ;

Who sitteth upon honeyed lips
And waiteth till he comes and sips.
SPIRIT OF LOVE, we hail thee! Come !
Thou Spirit of the young man's home.

'Tis Love from baby eyes that peepeth ;
'Tis Love with infant-joy that leapeth ;
'Tis Love with untaught voice that singeth ;
'Tis Love whose tiny finger clingeth;
In every infant look and sound,
Love, all-pervading Love, is found.
SPIRIT OF LOVE, we hail thee ! Come !
Thou Spirit of the young man's home.

In summer skies, in youth's sweet morning,
In every tint those times adorning,
In every odour that perfumeth
When every flower is sweet and bloometh.
'Tis Love produceth the delight ;
'Tis Love must to the feast invite.
SPIRIT OF LOVE, we hail thee ! Come !
Thou Spirit of the young man's home.

And when a short gloom hangs before us,
'Tis but a cloud just passing o'er us ;
Each drop which falls the cloud will lighten,
And does but help the sky to brighten.

E

Beyond the cloud and far above,
There ever shines the sun of Love.
Spirit of Love, we hail thee ! Come !
Thou Spirit of the young man's home.

THE SPIRIT OF THE OLD MAN'S HOME.

" My hope is in thee."—Psalm xxxix. 7.

SPIRIT of Hope, in age's dwelling,
Of peace, of joy, of heaven telling ;
Who makes the sweet hour taste the sweeter,
Who makes the fleet year pass the fleeter ;
Who, as life hastens to its close,
Shows brighter things than mere repose.
Spirit of Hope, we hail thee ! Come !
Thou Spirit of the old man's home.

Without thee, what were age's thinkings,
The mind's decay, the spirit's sinkings ?
The bowed-down frame, weak, aged, and shaking,
Would dread the parting soul's forsaking.
Who could withstand such years of fear,
With nought beyond the grave to cheer ?
Spirit of Hope, we hail thee ! Come !
Thou Spirit of the old man's home.

Yes ! Blest with Hope, though days were sadder,
Each were a step on Jacob's ladder,
An upward step ! The rocky pillow
Again may sink in passion's billow.
Each step removes us from the ground,
Makes more distinct each heavenly sound.
SPIRIT OF HOPE, we hail thee ! Come !
Thou Spirit of the old man's home.

But there are brighter things than this ;
See, expectation's lost in bliss
And faith in sight.   See, promise fadeth
In the great glory that pervadeth ;
'Mid one loud hymn of constant praise,
Through countless, never-ending days.
SPIRIT OF HOPE, we hail thee ! Come !
Thou Spirit of the old man's home.

THE DEAD MAN'S BOAT.

TO-DAY I saw a lifeless thing,
With shattered frame and drooping wing,
Now drifting here, now drifting there,
As winds or currents chanced to bear ;

Without a guiding mind or will
It drifted onward, backward still.
" What is it," said I, " that I note ?"
" It is," said one, " the dead man's boat."

" Whose was the boat ?   When was't he died ?"
I asked again, and then I sighed ;
For, I bethought me, when we die
How many things neglected lie!
The " trim-built wherries " that we prize
Are common boats to common eyes,
They drift about while still they float,
And each is but a dead man's boat.

" Whose was the boat ?   Why don't you know ?
The boat belongs to Long-yarn Joe ;
He isn't dead, but just as good—
He's like his boat, old worn-out wood ;
When first he had the stomach-gout
He took the oars and rudder out,
And left it anywhere to float ;
And there it is—a dead man's boat.

" Lawks ! there are many here about
Belong to those who haven't gout ;

I know a big old Parish Church,
That long has had the dead man's lurch,
Without one compass, rudder, sail—
A water-logged old tub or pail;
It drifts, just managing to float,
A rumbling, tumbling, dead man's boat.

" 'Tis sometimes full of old men's noise,
'Tis sometimes full of prating boys,
'Tis sometimes smutched with showy paints—
Whitewash makes seemly boats and saints—
And then, of course, it is pretended
That the old rotten boat is mended;
I'll wage a sovereign to a groat,
Whitewash ne'er saved a dead man's boat."

" Don't libel thus that boat, old sinner ;
There's yet some fine old timber in her ;
Replace what time has rendered rotten
With heart of oak; she's sound at bottom.
Caulk up her seams, make good her keel,
She'll centuries serve the public weal ;
There's not a nobler craft afloat
Than what you've called a dead man's boat.

"A stalwart crew, a manly mess,
Was granted her by good Queen Bess;
And William afterwards supplied
What tyrants Charles and James denied.
Again she's got a leeward lurch,
But once man honestly ' The Church ;'
No British sea will ever float
With one sham flag, one dead man's boat."

MAKING BABY LINEN.

A PICTURE.

 PRETTY creature, just nineteen,
With light brown hair, and soft blue een,
Red lips, with rows of pearls between.

A form with varied charms abounding,
Where Beauty's self might sit as crowned in,
Once spare, but now a little rounding.

A neck as white as drifted snow
Its curl-hid arch now bending low ;
Long fingers, trembling while they sew.

A little square of linen white,
Almost a kerchief size—not quite—
With two small holes, one left, one right.

That little square of linen is
The shadowing of a novel bliss,
Well worth th' expectant mother's kiss.

Ah, well-a-day ! will it be worn
By something which shall soon be born,
Or will no sunshine greet that morn ?

Oh ! when the fancied time arrives,
Will she, the happiest of wives,
Think the day worth a thousand lives ?

Will she, amid her new alarms,
See placed in her dear husband's arms
A new-formed thing of matchless charms ?

Will drooping eyes, suffused with joy,
See manly lips kiss a wee toy ?
Will *his* dear voice exclaim, " My boy"?

From friendly whispers will she gather,
That " of the two it's like her, rather,"
While Nurse exclaims,—"No, like his father ! "

When the small feet shall move about,
How often she will then go out!
The sun will always shine, no doubt.

And when her boy begins to talk
How pleasant then will be each walk!
Nothing shall such sweet pleasure baulk.

And when arrive his school-boy days,
And rightly he each lesson says,
How he will gain his master's praise!

And as he grows to man's estate,
With father's mind, and form, and gait,
He's sure to be both good and great.

Or if the first should be a girl,
He will find grace in every curl;
Each day will some new charm unfurl.

For if one moment of alloy
Should check the all but perfect joy,
He'll say, " All right, she'll nurse the boy! "

Thus stitch, stitch, stitch, the fingers play,
And quickly move on, day by day,
And thought-filled hours thus fly away.

Oh, may no disappointment mar
These lovely hopes, these hopes which are
Bright as the morning's brightest star !

May fingers move and never ache,
And future shirt and chemise make,
For future little babies' sake !

And may the babies come, and prove
Each one a little " treasure trove,"
Well worthy of its parents' love !

Thus may the pleasant world move on,
A daughter now, and now a son ;
And sometimes two instead of one.

A WORD ON DEATH.

(WRITTEN ON THE DEPARTURE OF MY NIECE SUSY.)

LISTEN ! and I will speak of Death. I have just left the dead ;
   Have touched the hands, have kissed the lips whence warmth
   and life have fled ;
Have decently laid straight the limbs, have closed the
   fixing eye,
Have done what dearest friends must do to those whom they
   see die.

I speak of death! Droop not the head, and donot think of
    pain ;
Have you e'er seen one die whom you could pray should
    live again ?
When those we love depart from us we weep as men should
    weep,
But who, e'en then, could ever wish to break their placid
    sleep ?

I have seen pilgrim fathers, worn, agèd, bowed-down men
Pass the last feeble moments of their threescore years and
    ten ;
I have seen youth in beauty droop, with all the world could
    give,
And wondered at the Providence which said it should not live.

But all the solemn moments that I have spent beside
The beds where those I loved in life and love in death
    have died,
Have been so placid and serene, sweet ceasings of the breath,
Without a pain or fear, they make me quite in love with
    death.

My father and my mother dropped like some well-ripened fruit
With fifty or a hundred-fold of goodness at their root;

And now, as sweet a blossom as e'er bloomed upon the earth
Has fallen with all its promises of purity and worth.

I pace the room (why darkened ?) and I look upon the bed,
And view the pale set features of the beautiful—the dead—
All cold, and fixed, and motionless, that smile for ever gone,
Which warmed to smiles and happiness all that it rested on.

For ever gone ?   That beauty, that sweetness, and that grace?
The virtue, purity, the heaven which beamed in that sweet
    face ?
For ever lost that goodness ?   No !   I would rather think
The moon, the sun, the stars above, the universe should sink !

'Twill live again.   SHE LIVES AGAIN !   E'en my beclouded
    faith
Already sees her triumphing victorious over death :
All light, all love, all innocence, her few slight faults forgiven,
Ranged with congenial spirits in her congenial heaven.

She lives again !   I feel it now through these fast-dropping
    tears,
She lives, and I shall see her despite these doubts and fears ;
There's not one noble thought which lights the humblest of
    the sod,
There's not one spark of virtue, but is a part of God.

POETIC SITES.

TOMB OF ROSAMOND.

THE tomb. of the world's rose!   And is it here
    That the fair Rosamond's sweet form was laid ?
Come, let us view it.   Now for diamond eyes
That set all hearts a-beating ; the red lips
Pressed by her king's alone ; the swan-like neck,
Hung with a nation's pearls, and not less white.
    Oh ! we shall see a smile which will enchant
Even the chilly heart of age to love,
A form which sylphs might envy, and a grace
And majesty excelling excellence.
Come, we'll remove the lid, and see for once
Embodied beauty ; for what lovely flower
Can match with the sweet " rose of all the world " ?
Yet stay !   Drink not with your strained eyes too deep
A draught of beauty, nor with unchecked gaze
Let your wild spirits wander, lest the sight
Of such perfection should unfit the heart

For future bliss elsewhere—
             See, it is—there!
A crumbled pinch of dust!
             A breath—'tis gone!
Never to be collected till the winds,
And earth, and seas give back their particles
To be re-formed. And is this beauty's boast?
A few years' reign alone, and is it gone?
Oh! if no virtue hallow the poor clay,
Regard not beauty. Penitence may yield
Its evening light, but 'tis a fearful chance
For us ephemerals to lavish day
Counting on twilight. Poor frail Rosamond,
Pity her fate and shun it.

SHAKESPEARE'S GRAVE.

IN THE CHANCEL OF HOLY TRINITY CHURCH, STRATFORD-ON-AVON.

THE dust of Shakespeare is enclosèd here,
    Here, by the very altar of his God.
From hence let all "for Jesu's sake forbear
To move these bones," which in less holy place
Were bowed unto and worshipped as becomes

Not man to bow to man.   But even here
Still let us pay the highest reverence
Which we may yield to genius half divine,
Nor let the fancy rove in a wide swerve
For recollections of his wit alone.
Let us not yield to Shakespeare's mighty mind
The stinted homage a mere rhymester claims.
Delightful moralist! with giant's grasp
He held the passions which direct mankind,
 And moved them all to virtue, showing vice,
Crowned vice, torn nightly by those "terrible dreams,"
Which make e'en conquerors tremble, and meek virtue
Happy, though compassed by a prison's walls.

   Shakespeare could jest, and prudery may frown,
But must confess he ne'er laughed virtue down:
But whether grave or gay, through smile or jest,
He led the heart to virtue and to love.

ON VISITING "THE THIEVES' HOUSE,"

WEST STREET, SMITHFIELD.

COME, rank, and see for once how vice is bred,
   Nursed, cradled, perfected among the poor;
See how for centuries the squalid nooks

Grow up among us ; adding, year by year,
Intricate way to way, till, labyrinthed
Secure at last, vice revels as it wills,
Deepens to horror and becomes sublime.

   Yes, with its perfumed kerchief, oft applied,
Rank visits *now* this scenic throne of vice,
Pleased at th' excitement ! and will leave the spot
And never ask, " How much have I built up
Of this sad monument ? "
                 Legislator, come !
Come, palace-housed! come, humbler citizen !
Come, ye neglectors of your fellow-men,
Triflers with man's great essence, who have starved
And dwindled down body and soul alike !
Come, read this bitter lesson. Know, that man
Hath power for good or ill ; the good shows first
In the sweet buddings of the infant's smile ;
Nurtured by kindness, it to virtue grows ;
But, checked by the world's cold frost, it soon shrinks down,
Concentring in itself, like the gnarled oak,
Terrible power ; and when next 'tis seen,
'Tis to repay, from some such haunt as this,
The wicked world's oppression and neglect
By pillage, or the wildness of revenge.

WALTHAM CROSS.

HAIL, hallowed monument of wedded love,
   That blessed remnant of the forfeit bliss
We lost with Eden. Hail, thou solemn tribute
Of Edward to his Ellen; sweet remembrance
Of a wife's love and husband's gratitude.
Hail, holy witness, that in kingly hearts
The milder passions may predominate;
That love indeed may nestle in a crown,
Scaring ambition thence.
               Oh, it is sweet
To turn from history's all blood-stained leaves,
To glow o'er such a tale; to see a queen
Participating in the kindly throbs
Which beat in humble hearts, and risking life
For her dear mate. What more could cotters do?
Read the bright page which hands the record down,
The sweetest tale that e'er was told of kings;
And let each manly bosom swell with pride,
That they were monarchs of the happy isle
Whose kings are men, whose men are almost kings.
Oh happy land ! where monarchs are endowed

With human hearts ; and use their sovereignty
To guard the circle of domestic joys,
Which British kings and subjects share alike.

HOLYROOD.

A GOODLY temple to the meek-eyed goddess—
  The soul-subduer, Pity.   Who e'er dreams
Of pomp, or pageantry, or princely halls,
Or royal ceremonials, by these walls ;
Who sighs for gauds, or breathes here a wish
For the poor mockery, greatness ?
                                        Sigh for her
Who, palace-housed, was yet without a home,
Twice diadem'd, who lacked the pearl content—
The priceless pearl which princes vainly seek.
Poor Mary Stuart !   Here in HOLYROOD
Was heard thy people's welcome to their queen ;
Here, too, the soul-entrancèd Rizzio drank
His draughts of love and beauty from thine eyes,
And paid his tragic penalty.   Here danced,
In gracefulness of form, the youthful Darnley,
Too soon to meet—but who delights to dwell
On such sad histories ?   Oh ! who would call

F

A needless tear into the eye of beauty,
Or for a well-turned period seek to move
With pain the bosoms which should rise with joy ?
Enough that here hearts high attuned for love
Sought the gay scenes of court-magnificence
For lasting happiness, and this vast palace
Yielded no joyous niche.   Alas for happiness !
'Tis not for time or place to mould it—No !

RUNNYMEDE.

A VISION of the past.— " I am a serf
  On English ground.   Oppression's chain has bound
And galled my limbs for thirty weary years,
Which I have pined away beside the banks
Of the majestic Thames.   Oh, while it flowed
So clear, so constant, and so beautiful,
Oft have I thought how blest a people were
Unfettered by its side !   How proud a spot,
Where to a port it deepens, 'twere to build
A merchant city, a vast mural fane,
To the twin spirits, Trade and Liberty,
Thence blessings to diffuse to all the world ;

And the wide world, no ceremony else,
Would own the rite by a loud song of praise."
　　A vision yet, for the serf's dream goes on :—
" The tramp of mail-clad warriors shakes the soil
Of Runnymede.　Ten thousand hands have fallen
On swords made bright and drawn for freedom's cause.
A shout of loud defiance fills the air—
A tyrant quakes, and, trembling, adds his name
To the Great Charter—one unworthy word
In the blest page of English Liberty."
The dream was prophecy.

THE BRIDGE OF SIGHS.

THE Bridge of Sighs ! the narrow-vaulted passage
　　Which leads the doomed Venetian to the end
Of his sad life of crime !
　　　　　　　And is it so ?
Sigh those o'er punishment who smile at crime ?
Mourn we, then, Guilt's detection and disgrace,
And would we see it rear its daring head,
Scorning the garb which modest Virtue wears ?
Alas ! not so.　Yet man may weep for man,
Though high the soul may swell at noble deeds,

And shrink from all dishonour ; nay, though justice
May sometimes claim the extreme penalty,
And its strong hand incarnadine, forgetting
The mercy all must ask, honour may yet
Weep over the dishonoured ; we may weigh
What natural weakness, chance, or circumstance
May have subdued to guilt, and give a tear
To our fallen brother on the Bridge of Sighs.

Cherish the whispers of the angel, Pity ;
There's not one feeling of the human heart
More purifying than the seraph breath
Which Virtue sighs o'er sin.

TOMB OF ABELARD AND ELOISE.

HOW wondrous the varieties of love !
With some, the stream glides on with sluggish pace,
Scarce rippling into passion ; cold and pure
Through all its course as at its virgin spring :
With some it flows as clear but more profound,
Calm though not dull, and constant though serene :
Sometimes it claims a wider range, and runs,
In its full current, onward to the sea,
O'erleaping all its obstacles.   With some

It swells, a mountain torrent ; raging down
Its ravined bed it drives its ruin-course,
Whelming, destroying all in its abyss.
　　Pity the unskilled mariners who dared
A wave so wide and wild.　Pity and forgive
Poor Abelard and Eloise : they lived
Their hour of wildness and romance.　Apart
They cherished in their inmost souls a love
Vain as the enthusiast's unsubstantial dreams,
Which fade with the first light.　Apart, apart,
Torn by the cold and ruthless world apart,
But not in death divided ; the fair forms
Which held their beating hearts lie crumbling here
Mingling in one dear sod ; and now, perhaps,
Their spirits, reunited, are rejoicing
That they are met again.　Oh ! ye young hearts,
Bear with your partings, for there is a shore
Where ye shall meet again to part no more.

KENILWORTH.

ALAS ! for the high eyries of the great !
　　Safer the lark's nest built upon the ground ;
　　Aye ! and more beautiful ; the lowly homed

Live a blest life of quietness and love,
While they who build upon an eminence
Build upon danger's brink ; the lightning's flash,
The tempest's blast, nay! a mere sudden gust,
May sweep to ruin.   Such Ambition's fate,
And of ambition my short story is.

    Once a fair dove wooed by a tender mate,
A fellow dove looked with ambitious eye
Unto an eagle's nest, and tried to reach it :
She left her dove-cote, and by a bold flight
Achieved her aim, and rested by the side
Of her new mate.   The lordly mountain bird
Was daring then the sunbeam, and the dove
Dared too its gaze, and fell.

               'Tis an old tale,
The dove was Amy Robsart, and the nest
Was the proud dwelling of the princely bird
Who built up Kenilworth.

———

TOMB OF JULIET.

TEARS for the Mantuan pair :
   To Romeo and Juliet give your tears,
    Tears hot as those on Passion's burning cheek !

Sighs from each lover for the slaughtered doves ;
Sighs deep as those which fan up Etna's fires !
O world, world, world ! cold, false, unfeeling world,
Must all love's votaries be martyred thus ?
O heartless, miser world, that wouldst not spare
Of thy wide limits but the little space
That such a pair required for life and love.

    Romeo, the young, the lover, e'en to love
Stronger than death or madness. Juliet too,
Our pretty Jule that " stinted and said aye,"
The night-masked maiden that dared tell her love,
And lived upon it till the merry lark's
Gay song seemed plaintive as the nightingale's—
Our own high-feelinged daughter of the south.
That chose her bridal in the chilly tomb
If it but gave her Romeo. Lovers, weep
Your hottest tears at this immortal shrine,
For hearts are here immured. If love, dear love,
The one pure passion of the human heart,
E'er homage claims, O Pilgrim ! pay it here
To Romeo and Juliet.

BAPTISM.

BY Jordan's flowing stream
   A mighty preacher stood,
One word was all his theme
   Alike to vile and good.
Where'er the preacher went,
His cry was still, " Repent."

His church the wilderness,
   Yet all went out to see,
Expecting as they press
   A mightier far than he.
" Repent, ye stubborn band,
Heaven's kingdom is at hand.

" Prepare Emanuel's way,
   Let all His paths be straight,
Already dawns the day
   For which His people wait ;
Repent, and be forgiven,
'Tis offered you from heaven.

" This Jordan as it flows
   Upon you thus I pour,

As pure as melting snows
  Descends the cleansing shower :
With water I baptize,
For water purifies.

" But there's a mightier One,
  The latchet of whose shoes
(The great well-pleasing Son)
  I dare not to unloose ;
His baptism is higher,
'Tis spiritual fire.

" The cleansing symbol I
  Pour on your outward frame,
But He will vivify
  Your souls with inward flame,
Will breathe seraphic breath
Where all before was death.

" His Holy Spirit then
  Shall warm each mortal breast,
And renovated men
  Wait for their God's behest :
Ruled by His gentle sway
A world will then obey.

"No more will then be trod
    The ways of sin and hell,
But all will look to God
    And strive to serve Him well:
Baptized by Heaven above,
A Baptism of Love."

THE LAST SUPPER.

"Do this in remembrance of me."

HE took the bread, and breaking gave
    To each surrounding guest;
From Judas, Satan's guilty slave,
    To John reclining on His breast.
"Do this wherever you may be;
Break bread, and then remember Me."

He took the cup and poured the wine—
    A cup of glowing love—
The last He tasted of the vine,
    Except the holier wine above.
He took the cup, "Do this," said He,
    "Let all do this, remembering Me."

The words of love were scarcely spoken,
    The cup was scarcely drained,

Ere the true bread of life was broken,
　And Calvary, the winepress, stained ;
This bread, this cup, where'er I be,
　Jesus, I'll take, remembering Thee.

I'll take the bread, remembering all
　The broken bread hath done ;
It is the bidden ritual,
　And mystery the rite hath none.
The bread of life Thou art to me—
　I eat the bread, remembering Thee.

I take the cup, for 'tis Thy word ;
　And as I drink the wine,
I drink, remembering Thee, my Lord,
　My Saviour, my Undoubted Vine.
Oh grant that I refreshed may be,
　With sweet remembrances of Thee !

A MAIDEN'S EVENING PRAYER FOR HER LOVER.

HEAR, God of love, a maiden's prayer,
　Sovereign of earth and heaven above,
Bless all Thy creatures with Thy care,
　But chiefly bless the one I love.

And, as we promised each would bear
   Their evening thoughts of love to Thee,
Hear, God of mercy, hear the prayer
   He offers up to-night for me.

GOD'S MANNA.

I FEED upon Thy manna, Lord,
The heavenly droppings of Thy Word ;
'Tis spread throughout the wilderness,
Each humble, seeking soul to bless.
May I one precious grain discover,
   'Twould fill Benoni's ample sack :
Is glory found ?   I've nothing over ;
   With but one promise I've no lack.

While morning's dews around are damp,
I go, alone, without the camp ;
Leave every worldly thought, and rove
To gather faith, and hope, and love.
With these refreshed, my soul, grown stronger,
   Travels its destined journey through ;
Weary, depressed, bowed down no longer,
   For Nebo yields my Canaan's view.

THE TRUE INCENSE.

"Let my prayer be set forth in Thy sight as the incense, and let the lifting up of my hands be as the evening sacrifice."— PSALM cxli. 2.

O LORD, when I would worship Thee,
 What offering wouldst Thou have from me ?
Will slaughtered goats, or sheep, or kine
Be fitting offerings at thy shrine ?

Thy shrine ?   The heaven's unmeasured space
Is thy unbounded dwelling-place ;
The cattled vales, the lowing hills—
All these a speck, an atom fills.

The world is Thine from pole to pole,
The circling planets as they roll ;
The worlds on worlds, seen and unseen,
Which are, which will be, or have been.

I dare not offer things so cheap
As blood of kine, or goats, or sheep ;
Nor censers whirl about Thy shrine—
The fragrance of all flowers is Thine.

Material things I dare not bring
To my eternal Spirit King ;
The best and fairest of the sod
I dare not offer to my God.

But praise and prayer, and truth and love,
Are worthy offerings for above ;
If faithful, they will please Thee well ;
Angels them equal, not excel.

Lord, at Thy feet I lowly bow,
Praise, prayer, truth, love, I offer now :
Accept these offerings, Lord, from me ;
My Father, I would worship Thee.

PSALM LXXXIV.

HOW blessèd, Lord, is Thy abode !
My soul longs for the house of God ;
There would my heart and flesh rejoice,
And constant praise employ my voice.

Where timorous swallows build their nest,
My peaceful spirit flies for rest,
Would learn its lessons from the dove,
And on Thy altar offer love.

Far better than sin's thousand days
Is one short hour of prayer and praise ;
In God's blest house the humblest things
Excel the pride and pomp of kings.

My King, my God, compared with Thee,
The world is lightest vanity :
Thy service, Lord, I would fulfil,
Would sing Thy praise, would do Thy will.

CONSTANT PRAYER.

A THOUGHT on God when day begins,
  Guards from a hundred thousand sins ;
A thought on God ere daylight sets,
Will help to pay our unpaid debts.

A prayer, as fades each lessening hill,
Secures His care to guard us still ;
Our midnight praise, unwearied yet,
Is heard, and guards of angels set.

Since constant thoughts, and praise and prayer,
Secure for us Almighty care,
Oh, be our lives one constant hymn
Of praise, or prayer, or thought on Him !

THAT WHICH IS GIVEN, GIVE.

THAT which is given, give !
　That which God lends you, lend !
Those who live by you, let them live !
　Be to each friend, a friend.

All have not gold to give,
　But all may yet be kind :
Whoe'er you are, where'er you live,
　Give love to all mankind.

WOMAN'S WORKS.

LOOK round the moving world and scan
　The great, the vaunted works of man ;
Huge piles of stone which seem to say,
We dare the progress of decay,
But ere is placed the topmost stone,
Decay has claimed it for its own.

The vessel ploughs with venturous sweep
The furrows of the billowy deep,

And rides with monarch flag unfurled,
The proud encircler of the world ;
But tempest-moved, the mightier wave
No more its throne, becomes its grave.

The river's bed, the mountain's mine,
Where heaps of golden treasures shine,
Are bared by man.   The glittering ore
Is added to his ample store,
But unenjoying the huge heap,
He dies and knows not who will reap.

Man toils, and on his weary face
The tears of care leave their sad trace,
As down his pallid cheek they flow,
And tell of trouble, want, and woe.
Man toils for nought, his work is vain,
Pain-bought, it purchases but pain.

But cheerful woman, far more wise,
Catches the moment as it flies,
In cloudiest hour perceives the sun,
Blest when a single smile is won ;
Extracts from even night a ray,
And with it forms a sunny day.

G

How slight the seed from which there comes
The happy harvest of our homes !
A cheering word and sorrow flies,
A smile, and lo ! farewell to sighs :
Affection's lips no sooner move
Than reigns supreme Domestic Love.

From what pure spring is it that flows
So calm a current of repose ?
Whose voice can thus at its sweet will
Say to all tumult, " Peace ! be still ? "
Whose presence sheds its light around,
And makes each fireside holy ground ?

Woman's sweet influence alone
Builds in each humble cot Love's throne ;
She bids us hold as meaner things
The pride of wealth, the power of kings,
Says " High-grown fruit is not so sweet
As the blest manna at our feet."

Oh, would we but be wise and hear
The wisdom of the Woman-Seer,
How full of joy, how bright, how blest,
Were then the world ! a world of rest—
A world where every pulse would move
To perfect bliss and perfect love.

EPITAPH.

HOW often death the feeble spares
  While he subdues the strong ;
And leaves the aged to their cares,
  While he removes the young !

A warning voice thus speaks to all
  Who hitherto are spared ;
None can avoid death's solemn call—
  " Let none be unprepared."

EPITAPH.

DEATH to the wicked comes with barbèd dart.
  With all the weapons of destruction armed :
The grisly phantom frights the strongest heart.
  The boldest sinner well may be alarmed.

Death to the righteous comes with friendly voice,
  And leads but to the mansions of the blest ;
He bids the feeble, mourning soul rejoice,
  He bids the weary come and be at rest.

EPITAPH ON AN INFANT.

I SAW at morn a lovely flower,
    Which shed the sweetest perfume round ;
But ere it reached the noonday hour
    It lay, a wreck upon the ground.

And this is beauty's fate, I said,
    No mortal power its charms can save ;
For flowers will prematurely fade,
    And loveliness thus find a grave.

But 'twixt the infant and the flower,
    How vast—how blest a difference lies !
The blossom passes with its hour,
    The waking infant never dies.

———

CONSOLATION.

THERE is a smile for every sigh,
    For every wound a balm,
A joy for every moistened eye,
    For every storm a calm.

Each sigh is sent a smile to light,
   Each wound in mercy given,
Each moistened eye will yet be bright,
   Each storm subside in Heaven !

THE THREE CHERRIES.

  " Well, sir, I am not yet so overblown,
    But I may hang some time upon the tree,
    And still be worth the picking."—TOBIN.

ON a tree, a little tree,
Once were little cherries three ;
Just had fallen the fading blossoms,
And exposed their swelling bosoms :
Pretty, pretty, little tree,
Pretty little cherries three.

As I viewed the Loves one morning,
With a blush their cheeks adorning,
Just as peeped the faintest streak
Fancy heard a cherry speak :
" I am ripened, fully ripe,
Please to pick me, I am ripe."

Soon I picked the little cherry,
But unripened was the berry ;
I ne'er touched my cautious lip
Even with this cherry's tip,
But 'twas flung away untasted—
Pity that it thus was wasted.

To the little tree returning,
Softened by seven noon suns' burning,
Brightly glowed the ruddy pair
Which I had left to ripen there ;
One, as then my pleased lip felt it
In delicious sweetness melted.

Summer's sun had long been shining,
And the autumn's tendrils twining,
When I sought again the tree
For the ripest of the three ;
But the cherry, long forgotten,
On its shrivelled stem was rotten.

Listen, maidens ; may not cherries
Lessons give as well as fairies ?
Don't then, pray, accept an offer
Because it is the maiden proffer ;
But, the first temptation past,
Mind you DON'T REJECT THE LAST.

THE CHILD WHO NEVER DID ANYTHING WRONG.

M Y maiden sister had a child,
    The sweetest thing I ever knew;
Its auburn tresses dangled wild,
    Its lips so red, its eyes so blue!

It had a straight and lovely form,
    And oh! a very lovely face;
Its hands (then red kid gloves were worn)
    Were always in their proper place.

It never once was known to pout,
    But the sweet creature always smiled!
It kept each little foot turned out,
    In fact it was a faultless child.

It never said a naughty word,
    It never did a naughty thing;
It was by its mamma adored,
    An angel, wanting but the wing.

It never ate a bit too much,
 It never asked for sweets or sours ;
Nor glass nor china did it touch,
 But sat where it was placed for hours.

When hurt it never sobbed and cried,
 Nor on the sofa would it loll ;
It well might be my sister's pride,
 It was indeed A PERFECT DOLL.

CHILDREN'S SHOPS.

OUTSIDE my garden door to-day,
 On a broad step just at the top,
Some little things, in their sweet play,
 Had formed and left a " Children's Shop."

Small bits of sticks, and pipes, and straws,
 And polished pebbles of all hues,
And nut-brown hips, and scarlet haws,
 And scraps that but a child amuse.

All these were spread in best array,
 As full-grown chapmen spread their wares ;
And here, no doubt, in childish play,
 Were learnt trade's lessons unawares.

A pebble with a certain spot
  Would purchase a less valued row,
And some rare crooked stick when got
  Would buy some settled length of straw.

A pinch of shrivelled leaves (best tea),
  Some rotten wood (an ounce of snuff) ;
Miss A. sold " so sheap " to Miss B.,
  " Two paper sillins,"—" twite enough."

And here they seem to come each day,
  And chatter their small bargains o'er ;
Still bartering this for that in play,
  Each morning at my garden-door.

And as I passed their shop to-day,
  Hastening to reach my larger store ;
Thought I, my work is like their play,
  Egad, 'tis very little more.

We trifles make and trifles sell,
  And get but trifles for our pains ;
At the play's end 'tis hard to tell
  The object of our petty gains.

From day to day awhile we strive,
    And then tired out, at last we stop ;
Such trifles charm us while we live,
    Ours is at best " a Children's Shop."

THE YOUNG WORKMAN.

(AN IMITATION WITH ALTERATION.)

IN a chamber next the sky,
  On a narrow and low stump bed,
Lay a little fellow, four feet high,
    Resting his curly head ;
His breathing was mild and sweet,
    For in health he was perfectly well,
But he started up and sprang to his feet
    At the sound of a factory bell.

" Oh ! it surely can't be so,
    It isn't already five;
O lawk," said he, " here's a pretty go !
    I must dress if I wish to thrive :
My eyelids seem to sink,
    As if I could lie till seven,
What joy I should think another wink,
    And another hour's sleep would be heaven."

Ding, ding, ding,
  Went the factory bell again,
The boy rubbed his eyes, and looked out on the skies
  Through his well-cleaned window-pane ;
A labourer bold and strong,
  Went by with the tools of his trade,
He sang aloud the well-known song,
  The song of the mattock and spade.

" Work, work, work,
  'Tis the duty and pleasure of life ;
Work steadily, work
  For yourself, and your children, and wife ;
The man who will heartily work,
  To his feet can boldly spring,
He need not wince at the frown of a prince,
  Or cringe for the smile of a king.

" Work with your right hand or left,
  Work with your shoulders or feet,
Work with your head, if a good one, instead,
  But work without any deceit.
Work, work, work
  For yourself, and your children, and wife ;
Work steadily, work,
  'Tis the duty and pleasure of life.

" To buy with the first-saved pound
  Of your well-earned honest wage,
Some long-wished comforts to surround
  The wife of your youth and age ;
Chair and table and bed,
  Bed and table and chair ;
On every one her smile is shed,
  And your work's reward is there.

" If one of a lowly band,
  Skilled artisan or clown,
If one of the lofty of the land,
  If the wearer of a crown,
Work honestly, work,
  Each has his taskwork given ;
Work, work, work,
  'Tis the high command of Heaven :

" Full six days shalt thou work,
  And all thy labour do,
Let the seventh be given to God in Heaven,
  Who six days worked for you.
The man who will faithfully work,
  May upward cast his eye ;
For if he lacked bread, the ravens which fed
  Elijah would bring supply."

In the chamber next the sky,
　　Near his narrow, low stump bed,
Stood the little fellow, four feet high,
　　As he combed his curly head,
And he said, " It is all very well
　　To rest till the clock strikes five,
But before the last sound of the factory bell
　　I'll to work, for I wish to thrive ! "

THE COTTAGE OF CONTENT.

I WENT to Chelmsford yesterday,
　　And though I drove eight miles an hour,
I spied a cottage on my way,
　　Which I had noticed once before.

And labelled on it, black on white,
　　I plainly read as past I went,
(The writer was a happy wight,)
　　" This is the Cottage of Content."

So it might be.   Its walls were rough
　　Slap-dashed, with lime-wash whitened o'er,
The door was made of homely stuff,
　　But shut and opened !   'Twas a door.

The cottage had a garden too,
   With beds for cabbage, beans, and peas,
Fruit trees and flowers it had a few,
   And just a hive or two of bees. •

The chimney smoked—so there was fire !
   Food, lodging, were each side the door.
What more could any man require ?
   With these one hardly could be poor.

" Well, really," thought I, as I leant
   Back in my chaise, and gave it speech,
" To me this Cottage of Content
   Does quite a little sermon preach."

Its happy tenant worked, no doubt,
   And had his livelihood to seek ;
He earned, by constant toiling out,
   At most eight shillings in the week ;

And was content ?   Well so he might !
   Let's see : rent, *three pound ten*, and then
Rates, taxes, *one* ; *two*, fire and light,
   Bread, *six* ; meat, *four*—£16 10.

Clothes, say *two pounds ;* drink, physic, *nil,*
 Books, sundries, *one ;* no debts, no qualms :
No fees or time for being ill,
 And just *ten shillings* left for alms !

Why what a stock of worldly lore
 Is in those two black lines of paint ;
A mine of wealth is counted o'er
 In this same Cottage of Content.

For there I read in language clear
 How each of us may live in plenty,
JUST EARN A FULL SCORE POUNDS A YEAR,
 AND LEARN TO LIVE WITHIN THE TWENTY.

THE PLOUGHMAN AND THE LARK.*

SWEET lark ! As breaks the day
 To each it labour bringeth,
  From morn to eve I plough,
  The lark the long while singeth.

* This is almost literally rendered from a prose translation of a
Polish song.

It is for me and thee
I give the land its dressing,
God prosper thee sweet bird,
Ask thou for me a blessing.

FLOWERS.

THE PRIMROSE.

HAIL, lovely visitant !   The Spring's first rose.
Not warm with blushes like the deep-dyed flowers
Of summer days ; but pale as the first hope
                    Of trembling early love,

When first it seeks return.   While, primrose-like,
It opes its blossoms at the Spring's first smile,
Daring to death the possible return
                    Of chilly Winter's time.

Alas ! the lover and the flow'ret die
Of coldness oft.   Sweet Genii of the Spring,
Guardians alike of earth's and the heart's blossoms,
                    Shield and protect them both.

Hold back the temptings of the sunny smiles
Which warm to unfolding the young primroses,
Till settled terms of sunshine have prepared
                    All for their dear reception.

H

THE DAISY.

BEAUTIFUL always, ever blossoming,
   Constant as is the dear 'enlivening ray
Which steals upon us in the " freshe morninge,"
   When it awakes and opes the eye of day,
Lovely throughout the year, throughout all years,
Whether in the Spring's smile or Winter's tears.

Unfading, never absent little flowers,
   Not planted here and there with sparing hand,
But scattered freely, so that the bent mowers
   May sweep their scythes nor fear to rob the land.
Ten thousand fall, when drops the latter rain,
And lo ! ten thousand blossoming again.

Beautiful deckers of the skylark's nest,
   Bending o'er each young bird a mimic ray
Of the blest sun, swelling its unfledged breast
   With dreams of heavenly beauty and of day,
Teaching the tiny warblers where to sing,
When a few weeks have strengthened each small wing.

Delightful Daisy, flow'ret of my youth,
    Thou bringest me sweet dreams of early joy,
Of unsuspected, unsuspecting truth,
    Of all that the man sighs for of the boy;
Thou tellest me of those dear happy hours
When all was beautiful as thine own flowers.

O, my sweet gem, my weary bosom sighs
    To tread the footsteps of my youth anew;
To fix my upturned gaze upon the skies,
    While clinging to my native sod like you;
Oh bear me to the daisy-studded vales
I loved in youth, my sinking spirit fails!

WALL-FLOWER.

NOT in the halls
  Of men, when garnished is the festal board,
    And flushed with pride, the castle's mighty lord
      Looks on his festooned walls,

      Not in the bower,
The flower-decked bower of love, Cheiranthus grows;
Nothing so humble there.   'Tis for the rose,
      Not for the poor Wall-flower.

Not in the spot
Where the trim gardener plants his favoured flowers,
To be admired a few short sunny hours,
        And then to be forgot.

No, lovely flower,
Thy blossoms smile where show has passed away,
Breathing their balmy fragrance o'er decay,
        Cheering misfortune's hour.

In pomp unseen,
Recluse thou stayest from the giddy throng,
An absentee from revel and from song,
        Shunning the gaudy scene.

But thou giv'st bloom
To the poor falling tower and ruined wall,
And in the roofless and deserted hall,
        Thou breathest thy perfume.

Like a true friend,
No smiling flatterer in a prosperous day,
But cheering and consoling when decay
        Tells of vain pleasure's end.

Go whisper, then,
Sweet Wall-flower, in each sigh of thy rich breath,
That Friendship's flower blooms o'er decay and death :
Go, whisper it to men !

TULIP.

F rainbow tints or gracefulness of form
  Could chain the sun-blast or resist the storm,
Or if the crowds which hang on Beauty's neck
Were fond and faithful after Beauty's wreck,
Queen of the flowers, gay Tulip, thou shouldst be,
And all would bow to beauty and to thee ;
But since, when past thy little day of bloom,
Thy fading beauty leaves us no perfume,
We dare not bow before thy beauty's shrine,
Or worship charms which fade so fast as thine.
Ah, no ! The beauty which leaves not behind
Some lasting charm, some loveliness of mind,
Some perfume of the soul which will live on
When grace of form and rainbow hues are gone,
May for a day our admiration move,
May please our fancy but not gain our love.

LILY OF THE VALLEY.

OH! what a lovely moral tells
　The Lily with its silver bells !
　'Tis said they ring on summer nights,
　Summoning all the fairy sprites
　To meet their tiny King and Queen
　Under the oak or on the green :
　If so, it surely is to bless,
　For how could Lily-bells do less ?
　Low in the vale retired it lies,
　Shunning the gaze of vagrant eyes,
　Close to its own dear parent earth
　It clings, the type of modest worth,
　But, hidden though in hood of green,
　Too beautiful to be unseen,
　Oft is it sought by those who prize
　The modesty which fools despise,
　Oft is it found by the fond few
　Who can esteem its virgin hue,
　And leave the flowers of gaudier dye
　O'er the sweet VALLEY-FLOWER to sigh.
　Oh ! is not this a happier state
　Than one short hour of pride elate,
　Than one bright gaudy, sunny day,

In blue and scarlet,—and away ?
Some may admire, but few can prize,
The flaunting flowers of many dyes ;
But I will seek the gentle one
Which seems the general gaze to shun,
Nor breathes its sigh of fragrance sweet
But to her lover at her feet.

Maidens, scorn not this humble tale
Of the sweet Lily of the Vale.

FORGET-ME-NOT.

DEAR flower, thou owest half thy fame
To the sweet magic of thy name.
How do we all delight to dwell
    On the fond hope that those we leave,
Those who have loved us long and well,
Will linger o'er our last farewell,
    And for our absence fondly grieve !
Yes ! each loved spot, and tree, and flower,
Will hear them at the accustomed hour
Sighing for those who used to share
The pleasures now but shadowed there.
Oh, Memory ! dear charm, which binds,
In lasting fondness, kindred minds ;

Whatever fate may have in store,
    Be mine a proud or humble lot,
Content, I ask or wish no more,
    If those I love " FORGET ME NOT."

MIGNONETTE.

ALL-FRAGRANT Mignonette,
    Where is thy honey-bearing blossom sighing
Its fragrance out ?   'Tis all around me flying,
Though I have searched long without once spying
    Thy little spice-flower yet.

    Ah ! darling, thou art seen:
Oh ! strange ; and does this load of honey-sweetness,
With which the air is filled to repleteness,
Come from a plant, whose highest boast is neatness—
    A little tuft of green ?

    Though scarcely more than weed
Thou art in form, yet never have I, surely,
Loved any bush, or tree, or flower so purely ;
Thy fragrance wins me to thee most securely,
    My Mignonette indeed.

Flowers of each form and dye,
Even from early youth have I been wreathing,
Each to be sweet and beautiful believing,
But in return for thy sweet blossoms breathing,
    I give my heart's first sigh.

HEARTS-EASE.

IN youth I planted a sweet flower
   Beside my own dear infant bower ;
  Its first blest buddings, all were noted,
  For on my little gem I doted.
  'Twas not a gay or gaudy blossom
  Which gladdened thus my infant bosom ;
  No flaunting flower the proud to please,
  'Twas but the violet flower, Hearts-ease.
  I loved it on from youth to age,
  It did my every thought engage ;
  Each day to tend my charge I flew,
  And, with attention, it so grew,
  So well repaid my anxious care,
  I had enough and had to spare.

Sweet reader, may I ask if you
Would have a stock of hearts-ease too ?
List to the moral of the sage,
" Plant it in youth, 'twill last to age."

SWEET PEA.

MY little fragile favourite, whither art thou tending ?
Where are now thy pliant little tendrils wending ?
Thy butterfly-like blossoms, why thus are they sporting,
Whither are they wandering, or what are they courting ?

I have seen roses bloom, I too have seen lilies,
Primroses and cowslips, pinks and daffodillies ;
Some excel in beauty, some excel in meekness,
Little flower, I think thy charm is in thy weakness.

Even from thy birth, of flowers or plants the weakest,
Long ere thy blossoms burst, a firm support thou seekest,
And as around thy prop thou thy small tendrils wreathest,
Oh ! all the sweetness there of thy fragrant soul thou breathest.

Sweet breath, sweet flower, sweet weakness ever clinging
To the one chosen prop from the beginning ;
Oh ! surely Love is here ! and, tho' shadowed but in flowers,
Each breath, each slightest tint of the " all-beautiful " is ours.

GERANIUM.

HOW oft, from distant flower to flower,
    Like vagrant butterflies we roam,
In search of happiness each hour,
Visiting every distant bower,
    Yet never seeking it at home.

Yet, there a flower of sweetest hue,
    Has grown beneath our early care ;
Its scent and beauty known to few,
Within our home its first shoot grew,
    And it has ever blossomed there.

Surely its perfume has not cloyed
    The sated or perverted sense,
Yet was its scent in youth enjoyed,
Though newer objects have decoyed
    Our wandering attentions thence.

Perhaps the summer shows us flowers,
    The sweet Geranium's tints to dim ;
But soon will pass the sunny hours,
And but a wreck will then be ours
    Of all that charms our vagrant whim.

Sigh not for gay and distant things,
　　For gaudy flowers no longer rove
They fly away on swallows' wings,
While ever in our cottage springs
　　The flower of pure " domestic love."

FUCHSIA.

BESIDE the rosy bower of Love,
　　Blest with the smile of sunny skies,
With sweets around it and above,
　　The drooping Fuchsia poured its sighs.

For the gay Summer time had past,
　　And brought no blossoms to its bough,
While Autumn plucked with envious haste,
　　The fading flow'rets from his brow.

Oh ! will the waning year pass by,
　　Scattering on all around me bloom,
While I, unblest, unfavoured, die,
　　No blush, no beauty, no perfume !

While ever-bounteous Nature pours
    Its rainbow loveliness around,
And e'en the wreck of summer flowers
    Strews with gay beauty the rich ground ;

Must I, poor unimpassioned flower,
    Thus coldly live and nun-like die,
Growing by Love's own rosy bower
    Without one glance from his dear eye ?

Just then flew by the wayward child,
    As thus the drooping Fuchsia mourned,
And the capricious urchin smiled,
    And to the plant his arrow turned.

The bolt had scarcely left his bow,
    Ere pendant pearls from each branch move,
Which, turned to his own tint, are now
    The emblems of "accepted love."

BUTTERCUP.

THERE is an unassuming mound   *
    O'er which I lately sighed,
    A step above the common ground,
    But hidden by tall tombstones round.
      Those lettered scrolls of pride.

This mound I planted with sweet flowers
   Of every form and hue ;
Transplanted from the garden bowers,
Which saw my Ellen's happy hours
   When I was happy too ;

The rose, the lily, the hearts-ease,
   And all the flowers she loved ;
The daisy, mignonette, sweet peas ;
Alas ! I robbed the village bees,
   And had them all removed.

I paced wherever we had trod,
   Collecting all she praised ;
With tears unknown to all but God,
I planted them within the sod
   Over her body raised.

I watched them all, yes, day by day,
   But soon each plant was gone,
For every night did some decay,
Till all were faded quite away,
   Except the humblest one.

But still a Buttercup was there
   To cheer me in my sighs,

And that to me, her worshipper,
One day seemed, *looking up to her*,
   My Ellen in the skies.

Checked was my woe, and shamed my grief
   As I the moral drew ;
It gave my sinking heart relief,
I felt our parting would be brief,
   And I looked upward too.

IRIS.

WELCOME, gay Iris, flower of many dyes,
   Twin sister of the Iris of the skies,
Bright flower-de-luce, fair bud of life and light,
Hope's own dear flower, sweet promise of delight ;
Strange that the tints of heaven's aërial bow
Should be reflected as a flower below.
But so it is.   Hope's tints are everywhere,
That man may shun the danger of despair.
True, the poor Iris of the earth is pale,
E'en the moon's rainbow tints too often fail ;
But a bright bow of mercy and of love
Spans the wide heaven, if we but look above.

How sunny bright the bow of Hope appears,
When the sky weeps its penitential tears !
Bound to my heart, dear Iris, ever be,
Blest shadow, of the tints I long to see :
Why o'er each little trouble should I sigh,
When the consoler, Hope, is ever nigh ?
What, though the skies may lower and clouds may frown,
Be not, my drooping spirit, thus cast down ;
Still are there whispers of eternal rest,
Hope shadows still the pleasures of the blest,
And every hue that cheers the failing sight
Is but a fraction of eternal light.
Come to my drooping heart, immortal flower ;
Cheer and console me in misfortune's hour ;
Point to the brighter Iris of the sky.
Strong in that hope no longer can I sigh,
I mount, I triumph, even as I die.

THE POPPY.

"FLOWER of the reaper, why so gaily dress'd
   In scarlet coat and spotted yellow vest ?
   Why dance at the first breath of each slight breeze,
   Whilst stillness sits upon the leafy trees ?

And why, thus gay and lively, not adorn
Our garden-beds, but grow among the corn?"
　　Thus to the Poppy.　Ere my questions flew,
Quickly were formed the ready answers too,
And ever thus can flowers a language find;
They wake to thought the lowliest, humblest mind.
　　" Poppies appear in smiling dress,
　　　　To show the charm of cheerfulness;
　　　　They stir with the first winds that rise,
　　　　To lesson us to exercise;
　　　　They grow in fields and lowly dells,
　　　　For chiefly there contentment dwells.
　　　　Oh! happy they to whom are sent
　　　　Cheerfulness, exercise, content;
　　　　The man with this sweet trio blest
　　　　Has found the talisman of rest,
　　　　And of the mystery knows the whole
　　　　Of the sweet Poppy of the soul."

HEATH.

THE Heath, the beautiful purple Heath,
　　With its blessèd brown stem; oh! I know it well,
With its gorse above, and its moss beneath.

I

There is not a flower like the purple Heath,
　　It bears, and it ever shall bear the bell.

The garden has its queen-like rose,
　　But the lady demands never-ceasing care ;
Whilst the wilding Heath on each bleak spot grows,
It makes the barren moors smile where it blows,
　　And freshens the breath of the upland air.

Garden flowers are for my lady's hand,
　　And each fresh one adds to a plenteous store,
But the wild Heath takes a nobler stand,
It grows on the unenclosèd land,
　　And blooms for the common's lords, THE POOR.

I love the Heath and so does the bee,
　　We both sip its sweets without asking leave ;
I love the Heath, for it seems to me
The very own flower of liberty ;
　　And that's why I worship it morn and eve.

The Heath !　How the beautiful wild bush blows !
　　The flower with the purple drops for me ;
The heather tells how freedom grows ;
And " the tint of fear," in its blossoms shows,
　　The purple Heath is the flower of the free

HONEYSUCKLE.

BY rustic seat or garden bower,
There's not a leaf, a shrub, or flower,
Blossom or bush, so sweet as thee,
Lowly but fragrant honey-tree.
By stately halls we see thee not,
But find thee near the lowly cot,
On latticed porch, by humble door,
Thou leanest with thy honey store,
Dropping, from thy bee-bosomed flowers.
Sweetness through evening's dewy hours.
Tree of the cottage and the poor,
Can palace of the rich have more?
No; for content as seldom dwells
In palaces as lowly cells.
Oh, I would scorn the mansion fair,
If pomp and pride and care were there,
And to the humbler cottage flee,
Leaving each proud and lofty tree,
For thee, dear Honeysuckle, thee!

SUNFLOWER.

FLOWER of the morning sun,
Thy worship is begun ;
  To bless thy anxious and impassioned gaze
Thy radiant god appears,
To dry up all thy tears
  With the first glance of his refulgent rays.

Flower of the noonday, turn
To where his beauties burn
  In splendour and in light, enthronèd high ;
He from his throne of gold
Thy service doth behold,
  And blesseth with his smile from farthest sky.

Flower of the evening sun,
Thy task of love is done,
  Farewell ! a last farewell to all thy sorrow ;
Constant throughout thy day,
Thy god in parting ray
  Promised to smile again on thee to-morrow.

HYDRANGEA.

"The beautiful blossoms of the Hydrangea are not its flowers but Bractea or floral leaves; they possess few of the regular organs of the flower, and could produce neither fruit or seed."

I OFTEN pass a leisure hour
   Within a neighbour's garden grounds,
And there is scarcely shrub or flower
   But I have noticed in my rounds;
And all I see I love but one,
Which I have marked, and marked to shun.

I saw its bursting blossoms rise,
   Of greenish white, a sickly hue,
But soon it wooed the sunny skies,
   And robbed them of their roseate view,
And with a rose's beauty spread
The bunchèd honour of its head.

And whilst it blossomed thus its hour,
   I saw the young and idle gaze,
They viewed the false one as a flower,
   And on it lavished their vain praise;
Whilst them it pleases, me it grieves;
Alas! its blossoms are but leaves.

They please the uninstructed eye,
 And charm perhaps awhile the vain,
But soon the rosy leaves will die,
 And neither fruit nor seed remain,
How can I then but thus despise,
Since all is gone when beauty dies !

———

SNOWDROP.

WHO knows not the pale virgin flower
Of winter's wild and chilly hour?
 When trees are bare and sunbeams fled,
 It rises from its icy bed ;
 Not warm with blushes like the rose,
 But white as its own parent snows.
 With drooping head and timid eye
 Averted from the passer-by,
 It wooes no love, it seeks no praise,
 Like the rich flowers of sunnier days,
 But heralding the coming spring,
 The SNOWDROP, pure and guileless thing,
 Shadows the pleasures which are ours,
 In childhood's unimpassioned hours,

Ere yet the heart has learnt to sigh
For long-sought, unfound sympathy,
While the bright day has brought no night
To chill, to wither, and to blight.
　　Oh, 'tis delightful to recall
The few sweet moments (sweet to all),
The blessèd springtime of our youth,
When all was innocence and truth ;
And if we only could retain
A lesson written us so plain,
How lengthened out to age would be
Our angel hours of purity !

MY FATHER'S BIRTHDAY.

SOME fifty winters I believe have shed
Their snows upon my father ; and he tells
That fortune has brought frowns as well as smiles.
His spring and summer, he has told me, passed
As spring and summer should, in joy and smiles.
Without a cloud upon the happy sky ;
And 'mid these summer roses and their sweets,

The first of newer blossoms, came his son,
And with him came anxiety and care.
But, father, though the later skies have lowered,
And the dark winter muttered out its storms,
Though all around were frowns, you still have smiled,
Yes, always smiled on me.   And though the cause
(The innocent cause indeed) of your new cares,
You have been kind to tell me that I brought
Feelings you would not change for all the joy
And pleasure of your youth.   O my kind sire!
I grieve to think I cannot dare to hope
That now when Fortune 'gins again to smile,
When my young spring and summer time is on,
I cannot hope that fifty summers more
You will survive to share this happiness;
But, sire, at least a few may still be yours,
And be it mine to brighten them.   You felt
A parent's fond anxiety, and now,
Expect at least a parent's recompense;
It is your due to see your labour's fruit,
And watch the blossoms of the trees you nursed.

Sad, that a heart formed like my merry dad's,
For playful turns, and smiles, and mirthful jests,
Should ever have been pained, and that his eye
Should lose wit's twinkle in full sorrow's tears.

I grieve to think that on my father's brow
The only lines which show are those of care ;
I would the merry wrinkle had been there
And smiles been on his cheek.   Well, well,
The past is past ; and though, dear father, now
I cannot smooth your furrowed brow, I'll strive
At least to keep all further wrinkles off.

    I often think upon my childhood's years,
And then admire the true philosophy
With which you met your cares.   When summer friends
Had left with fortune's smiles, you then could prize
The youthful circle of your own fireside,
Left with but few intruders, I paint then
Myself a lounger on your knee, my sister—
Always a favourite—courting father's smiles,
A younger sporting in your arms, enjoying
Its infant mirth at your assumed affright,
Or full of sorrow at the mimicked tear,
Feigned for affection's proof.   Such scenes as these—
Joys amid days of pain—I love to dream of ;
Spite of the sorrows they are pleasing still ;
And 'midst them I have seen my father look
On all the little objects of his love,
And then on mother, and with full heart say,
" Who, who can call me poor ? "

      No, no, my father,
You have an honest heart, a name unstained,
Not one to say, " You wronged me." You have all
The riches of your fifty well-spent years,
And those you still can hope for. For the rest
You have a happy wife to share this wealth,
Can you wish more ? You have your children too ;
Time must glide sweetly on ;
      And when, oh when,
My dad must cease to smile, and cease to sigh,
Then he can firmly hope, as hope I do ;
And I have nothing else to check the tear
Which rises at the thought, that at the close
Of his life's waning year, there will succeed
A newer, brighter birthday—a day where grief
Nor sorrow will intrude, but you and I
And all will ever smile. Father, adieu !

MY MOTHER'S BIRTHDAY.

MY Mother ! Oh, I dare not fetter down
My swelling heart with quips and turns of rhyme,
 When thus it beats for thee !
My mother ! oh, the burst of all that's sweet,

That hangs upon that one delicious word.
The first soft impulse which the infant feels,
When turning to the fond maternal breast,
Is to look up and meet the moistened eye,
And strive to lisp out " Mother." And when years
Have changed the lisping infant to a man,
There still is music in that magic word ;
'Tis luxury still to think and talk of " Mother."
And well it may ! From infancy to youth
'Twas you, my kind, my all-indulgent mother,
Who heard my little tales, and shared my griefs,
Supplied my wants, or taught me to endure ;
Who, if I have a virtue, gave it me,
And all my faults with care and kindness checked.
And since that time, whose heart but yours has shared
The tears, too, of my boyhood ? Who has seen
My days of sighs, when all supposed I smiled ;
Whose bosom was the pillowy sanctuary
Where I have hallowed grief ? My mother, say !
'Twas mother, too, for whom I penned my lines,
My heart's first glowings ; it was you who praised
And kept, with all a mother's care, my scraps :
Oh when, too fondly, you would praise my lines,
How proud was I to hear the honeyed words !
And if, oh if the happy time should come,

When I can say, " The gentle and the good
Have praised the wanderings of your poet-boy,"
I shall be proud indeed.
It were a pleasing task to number o'er
The constant glowings of my mother's love ;
But, where all's bright, 'tis difficult to choose :
In health, no opportunity was lost,
For a sweet proof of fondness and of love ;
But when your boy was on his bed of care,
And fever hung upon his parchèd lips,
'Twas luxury indeed.   To be assured
He was the happy object of such love,
Eased the sad bed of pain, and reconciled
All but the thought of parting : memory dwells
On pain, thus hallowed, as it would on joy ;
It is as when the queen star of the sky,
Through the dark night-cloud, shines in its full light.
It is so fair, so beautiful, so bright,
We, as we gaze, forget the ebon hours,
And only think upon the glistening gem,
And the bright heaven, from which it drinks its light :
So blest, so heavenly are my thoughts of youth.
There may have been a cloud in the blue sky ;
I think not of it : memory only yields
A dim but beautiful dream of happiness ;

Glimpses of sunshine, bright and undefined,
Sweet recollections of a rosy land,
Where every day was bright, and every tree,
Bending with flowers, each stream a liquid gem,
Each breeze a song, and every whisper love.
My childhood's home is my one fairy spot—
My "LAND OF THE IDEAL." And who breathed
The breath of love over this sunny land ?
Oh none but you ! Life, and still more than life,
The untired, untiring exercise of love—
The love of all I see in earth or sky—
Is all from you, who taught my infant mind
That I must love if I would be beloved.
Blest lesson ! blessèd lessoner ! Is there yet
Space for a drop in thy o'er-brimming cup
Of Christian joy ? Learn—oh, my Mother—learn
That but a fragment of my perfect love
Is yet known to thee.

A BIRTHDAY TRIBUTE TO MY SISTER ANN.

LONG has my harp, dear sister, hung
    Upon the willow bough,
  And but a brother's love had strung,
  Perhaps, it still had noiseless swung
    To winter breezes now.

Dear girl, our hearts were always one,
  Even in childhood's hours,
And union blesses still our home,
As when you know we used to roam
  And twine our gathered flowers.

Well, we can think without a sigh
  Upon our youthful years ;
For in the happy days gone by
We have not wet affection's eye,
  Except with pleasure's tears.

Mem'ry is sweet to those who live,
  As if their lives would last ;
And, Nanny, could I now receive
The brightest pleasures hope can give,
  I would not yield the past.

How could I part with every thought
  On which I love to dwell ?
With such sweet pleasures are they fraught,
That happiness were dearly bought
  In bidding them farewell.

The smiles of youth, and oh its tears—
  Its very tears are sweet ;

Affection still each look reveres,
And every word that love endears,
   'Tis luxury to repeat.

Do you forget, when full of play,
   We toddled down the hill,
What moralising friends would say ?
Yet many years have passed away,
   And we are happy still.

Time smiled upon our youthful hours,
   They glided swiftly by;
But still he strews our path with flowers,
He sears indeed our birthday bowers,
   But with the softest sigh.

And, as the future years pass on,
   If care our bliss alloys,
We'll snatch the pleasures ere they're gone,
Forget the sorrows one by one,
   And only keep the joys.

Each coming year will surely bring
   Some beauty to the mind ;
And as young folly takes its wing,
We'll keep the blossoms of our spring,
   And leave its thorns behind.

We'll keep, without the froward tears,
   The innocence of youth ;
Simplicity, without its fears,
The caution of our riper years,
   With all our childhood's truth.

And let us hope that future years
   Will smile as have the past ;
We have had much that life endears,
And hope as bright a promise bears,
   That happiness will last.

Of the dark threatening cloud of care,
   Let gloomier zealots tell ;
Most have of happiness their share,
Their days of sunshine in the year,
   If they but prize them well.

And though our spring-time has not worn
   Ne'er-changing, cloudless skies,
We still have had some sunny morns,
Roses have mingled with our thorns,
   And pleasures with our sighs.

What could we ask ?   I have seen those
   Whose lot has been as mild,

Sink under their ideal woes,
While we have borne the little blows
　　Of fortune, and have smiled.

Still let us smile.　A few more years,
　　At most a very few ;
A few more hopes, a few more fears,
A few more days of smiles and tears,
　　We bid this world adieu.

A BIRTHDAY TRIBUTE.

(TO MY SISTER PRUDENCE.)

WELL ! Years upon their circles whirling,
　　Are bidding Prue to doff her girling ;
I note the bursting buds are curling
　　　　Their blush-tipped bosoms ;
And soon, to summer's sun unfurling,
　　　　Ye'll see their blossoms.

But ilka bud is come sa dear,
To part wi' ane I dinna care,
I wish amaist to STAP THE YEAR ;
　　　　An' while I sing
O' simmer-joys, I drap a tear
　　　　To part wi' spring !

K

I paint ye oft the child I foun' ye,
An' s'pose your wee bit arms aroun' me,
Be sure a brither's luve has boun' me,
 For then, dear Prue,
Without reflect, I look aboon me,
 An' think o' you.

I think, an' have a thousan' fears,
O' baited traps an' hidden snares,
But then I think there's Ane who cares
 For sic as you,
An' He will hear a brither's prayers,
 An' guard ye through.

Well, Prue, sin' then the day's a-comin'
(I' faith already at its gloamin'),
When ye maun rank amang the women,
 Tak' muckle care ;
The boys will ca' ye a' that's bloomin'
 An' sweet an' fair.

But when these rantin' half-grown men
Admire your lip or praise your een,
Or whisper roun', " Her ancle's clean ;"
 I red ye note
Their 'pinion isn't worth a preen,
 'Tis a' by rote.

So min' what now your brither says,
It is by sic wee flattering ways,
They 'tangle maidens in a maze,
    And there ensnare 'em ;
They lead to ruin while they praise,
    So, Prue, beware 'em.

An' 'tisn't sparkling een, my Prue,
Or lips o' blush-tipped gowans hue
That's worth, my girl, a thought frae you ;
    They catch the vain,
But frae the steady thinking few,
    Na look they gain.

For when I spie a breast o' snaw,
An' see it rise an' see it fa',
The breath sa deep if feeling draw
    I strive to ken,
An' if sincerity's awa'
    Look na agen.

An' 'gin a drooping lid I see,
Moist wi' the tear o' sympathy,
. Ask I the colour o' the ee
    That gi'es the tear ?
I only ask ('tis a' to me),
    Is it sincere ?

Then, Prue, ye maun na care a piu
O' what's the colour o' the skin,
If brown, ye still respect may win
        By inward grace ;
If fair then min' ye dinna tin'
        A winsome face.

The chilly heart which never glows,
True pain or pleasure never knows,
Yours is the pulse which mounts an' fa's
        Wi' joy an' tears ;
But feelings sic as these expose
        To mony cares.

So, 'gin a sighing lad ye meet,
Who talks o' luve an' ca's ye " sweet,"
An' swears o' truth frae morn till niet,
        Ah ! then beware,
'Tis ten to ane it's a' deceit,
        To hide a snare.

For, Prue, amaist I drap a tear,
To say not a' the warl's sincere,
An' vice will virtue's maskie wear,
        Sa bold an' well,
That which is which 'twad pose a seer
        Aift-times to tell.

An' dinna trust in yer ain pride,
An' think 'twill a' your actions guide,
The best may chance to turn aside
    From virtue's path ;
For gowans deck the pathway side
    That leads to death.

Yet when (but time enow for this)
A laddie ye na tak' amiss,
Approach ye wi' a modest " miss,"
    I'll na reprove,
I know na purer earthly bliss
    Than weel-placed love.

But, girl, sic pleasure tasted early,
Without its pain is met wi' rarely,
Pleasure an' pain are mingled sairly
    In young love's cup,
An' tho' the brim may sparkle fairly,
    The dregs ye'll sup.

'Tis sweet, yes, Prue, I know 'tis sweet,
To feel a heart responsive beat,
To think a kindred soul you meet,
    An' gaze on ane
Ye canna' dream to know deceit,
    E'en by its name.

But plighted love grows sometimes cold,
An' dull the tale that's aiften told,
An' a' that glitters is na gold,
    Tho' sparkling fairly,
An' love that's neither bought or sold
    Is met wi' rarely.

Well, life, my dear, a sonsie dance is,
Where a' alike maun tak' their chances ;
While Fortune humours a' the fancies
    O' those she smiles on,
She aiften sen's her waur mischances
    To him wha toils on.

But, Prue, let virtue guide your breast,
An' leave to Providence the rest,
The path of virtue must be best,
    Though sometimes rude,
An' if there be the truly blest,
    It is the good.

An' sin' we cannot choose our lot,
Be discontent, my girl, wi' nocht,
An' 'gin a palace or a cot
    Fa' to your share,
It's sure to be a happy spot,
    So wish na mair !

A FATHER'S LOVE.

DEAR one, ere yet upon thy baby brow
　　The first faint dawnings of thy mind appeared,
I loved thee for thy own dear self; and now,
　　When love repays my love, oh, how endeared,
How almost idolized, my child, art thou !
May no rude wind shake from the lovely bough
　　The pure and fragrant blossoms of thy spring.
Oh ! may the great All-merciful allow
　　Nothing to stain my pure and spotless thing !
May every rising sun some bounty fling
On thy fair cheek, my pretty opening flower,
　　The pure and virgin white envermeiling
With each warm tint ; but yet from beauty's bower
Withhold each blush.　My child, be purity thy dower.

A MOTHER'S LOVE.

FROM the close-textured and deep-rooted trees
　　Proceed the light and sylph-like blossoming things,
Which the bright jocund eye delighted sees,
　　Decking the boughs in our sunshiny springs,

Gladdening the little honeysucking bees
    When they first see the peach-blooms ruby rings
Marrying the young sunshine and the breeze.
As light, as delicately touched as these,
    Art thou, my beautiful child ; and yet I trace,
Though writ in softest lines (oh ! how they please),
    The manly vigour of thy father's face !
He sees it too ; watches thee on my knees,
And says each day adds to thy form a grace.
O God, my grateful heart's too big for its small space.

A BROTHER'S LOVE.

TWIN branch, that with me budded, blossomed, grew,
    Each intertwined with each ; decking the bower
Of love, our home.   Sweet sister, how on you
    Has each fond thought rested since childhood's hour !
    Noting the deepening tints, as my sweet flower
Blushed into beauty.   First the rose's hue
    Glowed on your healthful cheek, a priceless dower ;
Then Love his tremulous tint of purest blue
    Shed from your eyes.   Unconscious of its power,
You then unwittingly its glances threw

Upon a passing stripling.   Happy hour,
If with its power of beauty, he then knew
     The all-enduring fragrance of the flower,
     He then had made his home an amaranthine bower.

GRANDFATHER GREY AND GRANDDAUGHTER GAY.

OH tell me, my dear little schoolfellow, pray,
If ever you saw my old Grandfather Grey;
     His face is so wrinkled, his eyes are so dim,
     Yet I never can think without pleasure on him.
     He kisses and calls me his Granddaughter Gay;
     You don't know how I love my dear Grandfather Grey.

How funny he looks when he munches his bread,
He scarcely has got a tooth left in his head;
     But since he can't eat the least bit of the crust,
     He must have the crumb—don't you think, dear, he must;
     And the teeth which he praises of Granddaughter Gay
     Shall eat up the crusts for her Grandfather Grey.

And though he can walk yet, and says he is hale,
He tells me that shortly his old legs will fail,

That his steps will soon cease to be nimble and quick,
(Already he asks me to bring him his stick).
If assistance he wants, here's his " dear little Gay"
Will be a support to her " Grandfather Grey."

I'll hem all his kerchiefs, the red and the blue ;
Oh dear, how I wish I knew something to do !
He speaks and he does all so kindly to me,
And I've nothing by which all my love he can see ;
But I know that he loves his dear pet, little Gay,
And he knows that I love my dear Grandfather Grey.

———

THE WILD ANEMONE.

IN some fair grounds in Charlton road
    I strolled with Prue to-day,
  And at one moment we both saw
    A wild Anemone.

We looked into each other's eyes,
    And they were wet with tears ;
We almost heard each other's sighs,
    Both travelled back ten years.

Ten years ago—the March was mild—
　　Ten years this very day,
In Hornsey Wood, a darling child
　　Plucked an Anemone.

With joyous care she brought it home,
　　As a stray precious thing ;
She did not know what loveliness
　　God scatters every spring.

I told the little which I knew
　　Of Nature's lovely blooms ;
I spoke of each wild blossom's hue,
　　And of their sweet perfumes.

How every hillock had its flower,
　　Which man might never see ;
How some might bloom but one short hour,
　　To feed one honey bee.

But though thus scattered everywhere,
　　O'er hill, and vale, and plain,
No scent was wasted in the air,
　　No beauty bloomed in vain.

Sometimes it pleased a sated sense,
　　While wafted on the wind ;

Sometimes a flower's more rich incense
   Made holier a mind.

Like angel flowers, for earth too fair,
   Which, ripened for above,
Had still a happy mission here,
   And shed their seeds of love.

Our darling smiled, she faintly smiled,
   And gave a silent kiss ;
She was herself (the precious child)
   Full ripened then for bliss.

And scarcely had the flower decayed,
   (That wild Anemone)
Before that pure and gracious maid
   Had from us passed away.

But each sweet look, and smile, and sigh
   Drops on us all around :
Oh, scattered goodness cannot die,
   Even in thorny ground !

ON THE RECOVERY OF A YOUNG LADY FROM ILLNESS.

WHEN beauty droops we mourn its sigh,
　　But ne'er expect its young charms' blight ;
We deem not lovely things can die,
　　They look so heavenly and so bright.

The breath that bids its pulses sleep,
　　Pales the sweet lip, and sinks the eye ;
But while we gaze, and gaze and weep,
　　We dare not think it e'er can die.

Like love's young dream we see it fade,
　　But 'tis so charming as it flies,
We follow still the lovely shade,
　　And hope may droop, but never dies.

Too often droop our loveliest things,
　　And stars will set and moons will wane,
But is 't in the heart's imaginings
　　That they will never shine again ?

TIME HAS PASSED O'ER HIM.

(AN IMITATION.)

TIME has passed o'er him like a breeze
  Which steals sweet odours from the flowers,
As floating o'er the blossomed trees,
It but exhales their essences
  To give them to the perfumed hours.

Time has passed o'er him like a ray,
  Which travels from the central sun,
Making, to all around it, day,
Brightening and warming in its way
  All that it rests or shines upon.

Time has passed o'er him like a mist,
  Which for awhile obscured the sky ;
But, rising from the earth it kissed,
Found the bright light which here it missed,
  And shines a sun-lit cloud on high.

NELLY BROWN.

SWEET Nelly Brown, of Tawstock town,
    Was but a cotter's daughter,
But dukes might praise her pretty ways,
    And princes might have sought her.
Her honeyed lip a bee might sip,
    A sylph might praise her form,
Her eye was bright as sunshine light,
    Her cheek as sunshine warm.
Oh love, love, love, if any one you know,
    Who refuses your sceptre to own ;
You may rule him with a straw, if only once he saw
    The face of my sweet Nelly Brown.

By Taw's green side, 'twas there I spied
    This pride of Tawstock village ;
To Barum town was mother gone,
    And father to his tillage.
One rapturous look I scarcely took,
    My heart to hers was flown ;
I sighed "relent"—she sighed "content,"
    And mine was Nelly Brown.
Oh love, love, love, if any one you know,
    Who refuses your sceptre to own ;
You may rule him with a straw, if only once he saw
    The face of my sweet Nelly Brown.

THE COTTAGE OF THE YEO.

I KNOW the greenest, loveliest spot
    Of all this green and lovely isle,
And there I know a lowly cot
    Which would from palaces beguile :
'Tis fragrant with the spicy sighs
    Which, nestling, lurk among the flowers,
'Till, fanned by bees'-wings, they arise,
    And for the cottage leave the bowers.

And by the cottage flows a stream,
    Which dimples into smiles each hour ;
Uncertain which to woo, the beam
    Of sun above, or neighbouring flower :
And, as it passes the dear spot,
    It seems awhile to linger by ;
Ah, happy stream to watch that cot,
    " No meddling world enquiring why."

Oh ! could you see at twilight's hour,
    When eve its first soft dimness throws
The halo round the rich sunflower,
    The softened tints of the red rose ;

You then would sigh, as I have sighed,
    In these secluded walks to go ;
To leave the city's foolish pride
    For the sweet cottage of the Yeo.

Why does the flaunting city fling
    A glittering chain around my heart,
When I would be a lowly thing,
    And but sustain the humblest part ?
Honours and wealth, I seek ye not ;
    With you I joy should never know ;
This is my one dear, chosen spot,
    The lowly cottage on the Yeo.

THE YOUNG KNIGHT.

THE bugle is heard from the castle wall,
    And banners are seen by the castle gates ;
" Rouse, young knight, rouse at thy honour's call ;
    Thy helmet is brought, and thy palfrey waits."
Thus sang the minstrel through the hall,
And the young knight roused at the minstrel's call.

The knight was checked by a snow-white hand,
    And a voice like music breathed out, " Stay,

Oh stay to protect thy native land !
 Not honour nor duty now calls thee away."
But the voice of the minstrel was heard in the hall,
And the young knight roused at the minstrel's call.

The young knight left his weeping bride,
 And a happy home and a honest name,
And poured out his proud heart's crimson tide,
 In the fatal search for a warrior's fame :
The voice of the minstrel was heard in the hall,
But it was to mourn over the young knight's fall !

OH, DRY THOSE TEARS.

OH, dry those tears, those pearly tears,
 Which now thine eyes are steeping ;
Oh drive those weak, those woman's fears,
 Which set thine heart a-weeping :
I ne'er, dear girl, could prove untrue,
 Your charms would never let me ;
How could I love a maid but you,
 How could I e'er forget thee ?
No ! If a smile from Beauty's eye,
 With luring bait, address me,

Then I shall heave a heartfelt sigh,
 And think upon my Jessy ;
And should I tread on danger's ground,
 And pleasure's lures beset me,
Oh ! then to thee my thoughts will bound,
 I shall not then forget thee !

RESTING TIME.

SEE, see, dear, the red sun is setting,
 And darkness, love's day-time, descends with its blessings,
The cares of the sunlight the world is forgetting,
 And its toil is repaid by the evening's caressings.
  Cease, busy head, now,
  Thy worktime is sped now ;
  Cease, cease, nimble finger,
  Nor wearily linger,
The daylight is dying, its work is nigh done ;
And evening, blest life-time of love, is begun.

Turn, turn, dear, thine eyes from day's duty,
 Leave their dull task-work, and turn them on me ;
Labour surrenders the world, love, to beauty,
 The bird seeks its nestlings, and so, dear, must we.

Hands miss their mark, love,
When plied in the dark, love;
The wearisome day-time
Now gives way to play-time;
For the evening proclaims that day's task-work is done,
And the heart and the lip say their life is begun.

———

SONG.

WHEN sparkles the first star of eve in the sky,
   Give a moment, dear Jessy, to me,
And think while you gaze on the twinkler that I
   Am then gazing and thinking on thee.
In the day for an instant your image may leave
   The warm throne where it ever should reign;
But, ah! at the love-breathing zephyrs of eve
   I think on my Jessy again.

Oh! eve is the time for all beauty and bliss,
   They seem to recede from the sun,
But at eve the bright god gives his Thetis a kiss,
   And the sweet reign of love is begun:

And though in the day e'en such bosoms as ours
Must from fondness or feeling refrain,
Yet evening, dear Jessy, has left us its hours
To think on each other again.

LUCY GRAY.

BEWITCHING Lucy Gray,
 See youthful lovers two,
Enchained by you to-day,
 For your decision sue ;
A willing prisoner
 For life is either beau ;
Decide which you prefer,
 And let the other go.

One offers golden store,
 And houses, gems, and land ;
The other is but poor,
 But comes with heart and hand :
Your choice, then, don't defer,
 Pronounce a yes or no ;
Decide which you prefer,
 Or else *they both will go.*

SONG.

YOUNG Love on the breast
    Of a fair lily lighted,
Its snowy charms pressed,
    And sang there, delighted ;
    But the young flower frighted,
From his bright gaze withdrew,
    And the gay boy slighted,
To another flower flew.

Round a rose-tree near
    A jasmine was clinging,
And profusely there
    Was its fragrance flinging;
    And young Love, springing,
Reached the jasmine flower,
    And still kept singing,
As pleased as before !

SONG.

YOUNG Love, when he flies,
    In tears dips his wings,
And his heart's first sighs
    Around him he flings.

The sad tear may dry,
Forgotten be the sigh,
For if once Love fly,
   He his farewell sings.

              Farewell!

A beautiful breast
   Love seeks, in the spring,
And builds there his nest,
   Like a foolish thing :
He may cling there and sigh
Till his young hopes die ;
But if once Love fly,
   Then his farewell sing.

              Farewell!

SONG.

WE saw each other but an hour,
   But what has time with love to do ?
An instant wakes the passion's power,
   And following years but prove it true :
Let duller souls than ours proclaim
   That time must fan Love's spark divine ;
A moment lights the brightest flame
   That ever glowed on any shrine.

We saw each other but an hour
   Beneath the soft, the moonlit sky ;
Could years of truth exceed the power
   Sweet Jessy, of your maiden sigh ?
The thrilling touch, the heaving breast,
   The sinking sigh, when sighs are true,
The birth of love, when love is blest,
   Oh ! what have these with time to do ?

———

LILLA'S LEGACY.

MY pretty little Lilla's dead—
   At least is dead to me—
But ere her gentle spirit fled,
   She left a legacy ;
She left me—days of countless sighs
   And years of sweet regrets,
A love, alas ! which never dies,
   A heart which ne'er forgets.

I, kneeling, asked a single word
   In token of her love ;
Alas ! my prayer was never heard,
   Her cold lips did not move.

" Leave me but hope, alas ! " I cried,
" If more you cannot leave : "
She trembled, pressed my hand, and sighed,
Say, should I smile or grieve ?

———

RIDDLE-ME-REE.

RIDDLE-ME-REE, Riddle-me-ree,
I love one and one loves me ;
'Tisn't for beauty, 'tisn't for pelf,
But each loves each for its own dear self ;
'Tisn't for this, 'tisn't for that,
And neither can say or think for what.
Riddle-me-ree, Riddle-me-ree,
What do I love, and what loves me ?

Riddle-me-ree, where should lips meet ?
Riddle-me-ree, where should hearts beat ?
Lips meet of course where others are meeting,
Hearts beat of course where others are beating ;
What should I wish for, what should I sigh for ?
What should I live for, what would I die for ?
Riddle-me-ree, Riddle-me-ree,
What do I love, and what loves me ?

SONG.

THE Torridge flows gently among its green valleys,
 And sings to the woods as it ripples along;
The wood-dove cooes over its musical waters,
 Where twitters the skylark its gladdening song.
But how can I list to the music around me,
 Or gaze on the charms it invites me to view?
Dejected, I dare not reflect on such beauties,
 Alas! I must bid them a joyless adieu.

No more must I sing on the bank of the Torridge,
 Waiting Echo's reply from the opposite shore;
Ah! no; I must leave the sweet stream in its windings,
 And list to the dreams of my fancy no more.
No more view the sun to The Wooder declining,
 And tinging the wave with its mellowing hue;
No more hear the low bells of Bideford chiming,
 Alas! I must bid them a joyless adieu.

Bear gently, sweet Torridge, these tears to my fair one,
 But, ah! that such weakness is mine never tell,
Breathe softly, young breeze, this adieu to my charmer,
 But say not who whispers so sad a farewell.

Farewell, ye loved hills, and farewell, ye loved valleys,
  Already ye seem to recede from my view ;
Dejected, I dare not reflect on your beauties,
  Alas! I now bid them a joyless adieu.

THE STORM.

WE sat upon the pebble ridge,
    Close by the bounding sea,
And oft I gazed upon my love,
    And oft she gazed on me ;
And never smiled the leaping main
    So sweetly at the storm,
And never shall I love again
    So wildly or so warm.

We sat upon the pebble ridge,
    And there declared our love,
And all was passionate below
    And beautiful above :
How the delicious moments flew,
    We knew but love's sweet power,
We took the moments pleasure threw,
    Nor looked beyond the hour.

We sat upon the pebble ridge,
  And heard the breakers roar,
And oft my charmer told her love,
  And oft of truth I swore.
The wild winds sang around our head,
  The waves rolled at our feet,
Romantic love ne'er formed a bed
  More wild, more purely sweet.

We sat upon the pebble ridge,
  The time flew swiftly on,
And oft we wondered why so soon
  That eve of bliss was gone.
But suns, alas! have slowly set,
  Since last I saw her form,
And never can my heart forget
  Our farewell in the storm.

———

NIGHT SONG.

SLEEP not, love, oh sleep not,
Thy soul in poppies steep not,
  Let thy lover weep not
    A moment's loss of thee.

Thine eyelids, love, are closing,
I dread their short reposing,
Oh ! say, if when unclosing,
    They then will turn to me.

Give thy rosy lips, love,
'Tis thy Jessy sips, love,
The moon scarce Chidley tips, love,
    Then why let slumber creep.
But at the morning's break, love,
I still shall be awake, love,
Oh, then but kindly speak, love,
    And sleep now, prithee, sleep.

THE ROSEBUD.

ENCUMBERED oft with pressing dews,
    The rosebud droops in seeming sorrow,
Yet soon resumes its former hues,
    Nay blooms more beauteous on the morrow.

So love though oft depressed by fears,
    And doomed awhile to sigh and languish,
Will yet shake off its dewy tears,
    And bloom the sweeter for its anguish.

SONG.

HAVE I found it ?   Yes, yes, 'tis a heart,
    A young warm heart !
With the jewel I never can part,
    No, never can part !
There may be doubtless many who prize
The laughing light of beautiful eyes,
And some who say ruby, pouting lips,
All other beauties and charms eclipse :
   Eyes may bless,
   Lips may press,
But they're nothing without the heart.

Oh ! when you find a heart,
    A warm true heart,
With the treasure never part,
    Never, never part !
Eyes may grow dim as they grow old,
And even ruby lips become cold,
But hearts once touched with the holy flame
Of love are ever and ever the same ;
   And eyes will bless,
   And lips will press,
When they're bid to do so by the heart.

THE PROPHETIC BOAT.

> " Those only can tell
> Who have loved as young hearts can love so well,
> How the pulses will beat, and the cheek will be dyed
> When they have some LOVE AUGURY tried."
>
> L. E. L.

I'LL form a little boat
   And give it to the gale,
A cork shall be its float,
   An ivy-leaf its sail.
        Sing heigh-ho willow,
        My boat is on the billow.

Steadily, sweet boat, glide,
   And prithee, backward turn,
Borne homeward by the tide,
   Foretell my love's return.
        Sing heigh-ho willow,
        My boat is on the billow.

Bright did the moonbeams play,
   My hopes as brightly shone,
But ah ! that last sad ray
   Showed bark and hopes are gone.
        Sing heigh-ho willow,
        The grave shall be my pillow.

LIBERTY.

SHALL the bird fly from tree to tree ?
  Shall the beast roam from wood to wood ?
Shall finny wanderers cleave the sea,
  And revel in the briny flood?
Shall these—shall nature all be free,
And only man want liberty ?

Man has the eagle's daring soul,
  The lion's great and generous heart ;
Search land and sea from pole to pole,
  Man is great Nature's noblest part.
Nature was made for man, but he,
Alone of all, wants liberty !

Alas, all nature lives on prey,
  Each hunts his weaker fellow down ;
Brute feeds on brute, except that they
  Seek other kinds and spare their own ;
Man follows man !   The weakest flee,
And yield their life, their liberty.

Curse on the cravens !   Whither fly?
   The flying wretch must be a slave ;
Thou or thy tyrant, man, should die,
   Thy footprint, see ! marks out his grave.
Strike now the blow !   Who dies ? 'tis he !
Take thy reward—'tis Liberty.

TO THE TRICOLOUR.

UP with the flag of Liberty,
   Up with the white, the blue, the red,
Pay honour to the sacred three
   For which our fallen friends have bled.
We offer Freedom's foes the white,
   We seek not war, but *must* be free ;
Refused, we to the blue unite,
   And steep our hands, deep-red, in thee.
      Up with the three
      Bright tints of liberty,
The white, the red, and the true blue—
'Tis Freedom's flag !   Let all be true.

Wave till the foes of Freedom fall,
    Till comforts reach the poor man's cot,
Wave o'er the proud's devoted hall,
    And traceless leave the hated spot ;
Come, plant it here, no fitter place
    Than where the poor have been oppressed.
Each flag waves o'er a ruin-trace,
    A traitor's home, a tyrant's nest.
        Up with the three
        Bright tints of liberty,
The white, the red, and the true blue :
'Tis Freedom's flag !   Let all be true.

TWO THOUSAND YEARS AGO.

TOWARDS the great, and wise, and good,
    We sometimes deem the progress slow ;
But let us think how the world stood
    About two thousand years ago.
Though we, a poor short-sighted race,
    Deem a long term two thousand years,
How insignificant the space
    In the wide range of Time appears !

Two thousand years ago ! Just when
  " Great Julius " heard that o'er the waves
There was an isle where savage men
  Ate acorns, and who dwelt in caves.
On Colne's and a few sedgy banks,
  Were some poor towns which scarce had names,
And a few huts, in feeble ranks,
  Fringed the wide marshes of the Thames.

Then Cromlechs and gaunt Druid rings
  From Kent to Sarum held their fires,
And men, at once their priests and kings,
  Harshly controlled our savage sires.
An unknown God demanded then
  Man's blood in bloody rites to flow ;
No GOD OF LOVE was known to men
  A short two thousand years ago.

Just then " the mighty Julius fell,"
  And while " Augustus taxed the world "
To us a Child was born, and hell
  Was countless fathoms deeper hurled.
And at the very instant rose
  London ! the central dwelling-place
Of men born to subdue God's foes,
  And publish to the world His grace.

The wondrous city was at first
  But a mis-shapen mass of wall,
Yet in the uncouth heap was nursed
  The spirit that must rule us all.
To London came the blest decree
  Which swelled the sun-lit arc above,
The Christian Land of Liberty
  Shall preach the Christian mission—" Love."

Heaven moves not as we creatures move,
  By impulses now good, now ill ;
God's ways are always ways of love,
  But His own times His plans fulfil.
Two thousand years ago high Heaven
  Proclaimed redemption's world-wide plan ;
Two thousand more perhaps are given
  To the wide-wandering tribes of man.

Evil and good in mighty war
  With us as with the world have fought,
Ill sometimes has eclipsed our star,
  The bright, the morning star of thought.
But clouds and darkness, and their powers,
  Though sometimes striving for the sway,
Will soon recede.   It must be ours
  To be dispensers of the day !

O England ! " To thyself be true,"
　　Each idol in thy camp throw down ;
One Book, one Priest, one God in view,
　　Take up at once thy cross and crown.
Error may strive, but strives in vain,
　　Thou sword and crozier may'st defy ;
O'er thee the King of kings shall reign
　　In never-failing dynasty.

MY YOUNG NEIGHBOUR.

OFTEN I look upon his lovely face,
　　T he seat of joy and gentleness and grace ;
H ealth traced in beauty's tintings from the rose
O n his warm cheek, and on his red lip glows.

B y all admired, let thy sweet face, dear boy,
I n rosy tints still paint a heart's bright joy ;
A s years pass on may no ungentle gale
N ip the sweet bud, or bid the blossom fail ;
C are day by day attends the growing shoot,
H ope's watchful hours expect thy pleasant fruit.
I n truth, what else, dear boy, can come from such a
　　root ?